Millionaire
Under the Mistletoe

TESSA RADLEY

First published in Great Britain 2010
Large Print edition 2010
Harlequin Mills & Boon Limited,
Eton House, 18-24 Paradise Road,
Richmond, Surrey TW9 1SR

© Tessa Radley 2009

ISBN: 978 0 263 22154 1

Harlequin Mills & Boon policy is to use papers that are natural, renewable and recyclable products and made from wood grown in sustainable forests. The logging and manufacturing process conform to the legal environmental regulations of the country of origin.

Printed and bound in Great Britain
by CPI Antony Rowe, Chippenham, Wiltshire

TESSA RADLEY

loves travelling, reading and watching the world around her. As a teen Tessa wanted to be an intrepid foreign correspondent. But after completing a bachelor of arts degree and marrying her sweetheart she became fascinated with law and ended up studying further and practising as a lawyer in a city practice.

A six-month break travelling through Australia with her family reawoke her yen to write. And life as a writer suits her perfectly; travelling and reading count as research, and as for analysing the world…well she can think, "what if", all day long. When she's not reading, travelling or thinking about writing, she's spending time with her husband, her two sons or her zany and wonderful friends. You can contact Tessa through her website, www.tessaradley.com.

For my beloved Sophie—
The world has lost an angel
I will remember your love forever

One

Callum halted at the threshold, his attention riveted on the woman pacing in front of the reception desk. The slanting rays from a lofty skylight caught her hair and turned it into a nimbus of glowing gold.

He took a step forward.

"Callum Ironstone demanded my presence here at three o'clock." She cocked her wrist and glanced at a serviceable watch. "It's already ten past. How much longer does he intend to keep me cooling my heels?" Her husky voice held an edge of impatience.

Callum stilled as her words penetrated. *This was Miranda Owen?*

Not possible.

His gaze tracked up from slender ankles encased in sheer black hose along the sleek lines of the narrow black, hip-hugging skirt. A black polo-neck sweater emphasized the indent of her waist and a saffron-colored coat hung over her arm.

Callum stared.

Digging deep into his memories produced an image of a plump teenager, more at home in a baggy sweatshirt, jeans and muddied yellow Wellingtons. The sunlit locks held no resemblance to the long, untidy ponytail. No doubt the braces were gone, too.

He cleared his throat.

She spun around. Wide caramel-brown eyes met his. His stomach tightened as he took in the lambent hostility.

One thing hadn't changed. Miranda Owen still blamed him for her father's death.

Callum didn't let the knowledge show as he

crossed the marble tiles, toasty from the state-of-the-art under-floor heating system. "Miranda, thank you for coming in."

"Callum."

That one snapped-out word hinted at long-held resentments.

He stretched out a hand. For a moment he thought she was going to refuse to take it. Then with a small sigh she relented.

Her fingers were strong, her grip firm, yet her skin was soft against his. Before he could come to terms with the interesting dichotomy of her touch, she pulled away.

"Why did you want to see me?"

A woman who got straight to the point—he liked that. Callum shook himself free of the bemusement that this grown-up Miranda evoked. "Let's talk in my office. Would you like a cup of coffee?"

A picture flickered across his mind of a three-year-younger Miranda spooning several teaspoons of sugar into a cup of hot chocolate at her father's funeral.

"No, thanks." Her reply was clipped.

He glanced across to the receptionist. "Bring Ms. Owen a hot chocolate and I'll have coffee. Bring some extra sugar," he tacked on before placing his hand under Miranda's elbow and steering her along the corridor and into his spacious office.

"I'm not a child." She slanted him a look from beneath ridiculously long lashes, and a frisson of awareness startled Callum. "And I no longer drink chocolate."

"I can see you're not a child," Callum drawled, giving her a slow, sweeping perusal. "You've changed."

"You haven't." Miranda broke free of his hold and stepped away.

Still truculent. The heat of desire receded. "Maybe I'm mistaken," he mused. "I'd gotten the notion you'd grown up."

Chagrin filled her face. "I'm sorry."

Callum doubted she regretted her lack of courtesy. Yet when her gaze met his again, he read apprehension in the wide eyes. What was she frightened about? Even as he watched, she straightened her spine and the moment of vulnerability vanished.

He waved to the two boxy leather sofas facing each other under an immense wooden bookshelf packed with books. A tall Christmas tree covered with red bows and silver balls reminded Callum that it was the season of reconciliation. But Miranda's frozen face warned him that reconciliation was the last thing on her mind. And how could he blame her? Feeling carefully for words, he said, "Look, let's start over."

Ignoring him, Miranda passed the cozy seating arrangement heading for a round walnut conference table beside a wall of glass, where she slung her coat and black bag over the closest of the four chairs in a militant fashion.

Okay, so she was going to play this tough, all business. Callum gave a mental shrug and seated himself opposite her. "I asked you to come in because I have a proposition for you."

"A proposition?" Confusion clouded her features. "For me?"

He rocked his chair back. "You're a chef, right?" Hell, he knew she was—he'd paid for every cent of her exclusive training. Though he'd been surprised to learn she'd used her qualifications to gain employment at a popular pub chain rather than some fashionable, upmarket café or boutique hotel. Before she could question how he knew she was a chef, he added, "Adrian told me you work at one of The Golden Goose outlets."

He'd stopped to inquire how young Adrian was getting along as a temporary driver for the company. The young man had been grateful for the vacation job and had revealed that Miranda dreamed of one day starting her own catering business. That had given Callum the perfect solution…a way to wipe Miranda Owen from his conscience forever. He gave her his most charming grin.

"Yes," she said guardedly.

She certainly wasn't blowing him away with an effusive response. Tipping his chair back to earth, he leaned forward and planted his elbows on the conference table. "Here's the deal. I plan to invite the outgoing chairman of a company Ironstone Insurance has recently taken over to a private dinner party at my home on Saturday night."

"He'll come?"

"Oh, yes. Gordon's staying on as a shareholder and I want to introduce him to the other directors. It's a celebration."

The melting brown eyes hardened. "I suppose that makes sense. Your brothers will want to get on side with a significant shareholder."

Callum stopped smiling. The merger had been *his* initiative—a successful one that would give Ironstone Insurance a strategic advantage over their competitors for years to come. And Gordon Harris had been even hungrier for the merger than the Ironstone family. Gordon wanted to retire, to take it easy. But Miranda's words stopped Callum from confessing that there was another, more celebratory reason for the dinner. That would only lead to a dig about protecting his assets.

Two fine lines furrowed her brow. "When you say Saturday…do you mean this week?" At his nod the lines deepened. "That doesn't leave much time."

He'd intended to railroad her into agreeing… and not leave any time for second thoughts.

"You don't think you can do it?" he challenged.

Angry fire kindled in the caramel eyes. "How many people?"

Hiding a grin of triumph, Callum rose to his feet and retrieved a manila folder from the polished expanse of his desk. Returning to the conference table, he dropped the file in front of her. "The details are all in there."

If he could start Miranda on the road to success, introduce her to some people, perhaps he'd be able to forget the hatred a pair of eighteen-year-old eyes had once held….

Or at least that had been the plan.

But having met Miranda again, he had a suspicion it wasn't going to be nearly that simple.

Standing behind her, all too conscious of the subtle fragrance of warm vanilla she exuded, Callum watched her elegant fingers flip the file open to the first page of the agreement his PA had prepared. Her shoulders stiffened as she read the figure he proposed to pay for a one-night job.

Satisfaction swept through him. She wouldn't refuse. His offer was too good. Helping Miranda get started in a business that must presently be nothing more than an impossible dream would be the perfect way to excise the disturbing memory of the wild accusations she'd flung at him.

You killed my father.

Of course he knew he hadn't, didn't he? Thomas Owen had killed himself once he realized there would be a trial—where he would almost certainly be found guilty on the overwhelming evidence against him. The courts showed no mercy against employees who stole from their employers. Thomas Owen would have known he was facing prison.

Yet Thomas's suicide had shaken Callum more than he cared to admit, leaving him haunted by a long shadow of guilt.

A legacy that he was determined to shake.

* * *

The black-and-white print on the paper in front of her blurred. Miranda was no longer aware of the maple-wood furniture, or Callum's spacious office. Instead she experienced again the hot ball of misery that had burned constantly in her chest from the moment her father's PA had called with the news of her father's arrest.

Impossible.

But her father's assistant had insisted it was true: the police had been, and had taken her father away. Miranda needed to get hold of her mother urgently. Callum Ironstone would be issuing a press statement soon.

At barely eighteen, Miranda's first sighting of Callum Ironstone on television had swung rapidly from interest in the handsome devil with dark hair, a sensual mouth and eyes that held a mesmerizing intensity, to hatred when she'd heard what he had to say. The press statement had been brief but damning.

All of it lies. By the time it came to an end, Miranda was numb with disbelief.

There had been a mistake. Yet Callum Ironstone clearly didn't believe that. Rage had set in. Her father was *not* a thief.

Her father was granted bail, and emerged from the courthouse pale, shaken, but determined to clear his name. He had done nothing to justify the indignity the Ironstones had heaped upon him after two decades loyal service. Miranda had been confident it would all be sorted out.

But what followed had been traumatic. And, in the end, Thomas Owen simply gave up. Miranda could still remember the set, serious face of the policewoman who'd knocked on the door to break the news that her father was dead.

Then came the funeral. Miranda's hands grew clammy and nerves fluttered in her stomach at the memory of the last terrible occasion she'd seen Callum Ironstone—it still made her cringe. Devastated by her father's death, her white-hot hatred boiling over, she'd confronted him in the stone-walled forecourt of the church.

The men beside him moved to cut her off. But she barged past them. Standing in front of

Callum, she inspected him with angry eyes. "How could you take a good man's life and destroy it?" she'd challenged.

His jaw had set, and his face had grown harder than the marble tombstones in the churchyard. "He stole money from me."

"So you decided to teach him a lesson and humiliate him?"

A flush seared his carved cheekbones.

A man who resembled Callum—a brother perhaps—stepped forward. "Wait a minute, young lady—"

She brushed him aside, focusing all her emotion on Callum. "You killed him. You know that?" Tears of rage and pain spilled onto her cheeks. "He worked for you for twenty years, you gave him a gold watch, yet you never gave him a chance?"

Her father had been given no opportunity to avow his innocence. Callum had relentlessly pushed the police to the conclusion he'd wanted.

"You're overwrought," he said dismissively.

That made the ball of anger swell inside her.

"And what's going to happen to my mother, my brother?" *Me?* "Now that you've destroyed our family?"

Callum gave her a stony stare. He raised a dark, devilish eyebrow and asked sardonically, "Finished?"

She hadn't been. Not by a long shot. But before she could vent any more he'd cut her off, snapping "Grow up" in a supercilious, condescending way that made her feel childishly inadequate.

Callum's words had been unkindly prophetic. She'd *had* to grow up, and quickly. Much as Miranda loved her mother, she knew Flo could never be practical. Overnight Miranda had become the adult in the home. There'd been no choice.

And now that same man was trying offer her money. A bribe?

"No."

Miranda felt Callum Ironstone start as she spoke. The sensitive skin of her nape prickled. A moment later a pair of bright blue eyes glared down at her. She'd never noticed their color before.

"What do you mean 'No'?"

Closing the folder with a snap, Miranda slammed it down against the glossy wood. "I mean I have no intention of accepting your blood money."

"Blood money?" he said softly, dangerously, and his gaze narrowed to an intimidating glitter.

She refused to be cowed. "Yes, blood money for what you did to my father."

"Your father *stole* from Ironstone Insurance."

Miranda shook her head. "You got the wrong man."

"Give me strength." Callum made a sharp, impatient sound. "You're not a child anymore."

"Stop it!" She put her hands over her ears.

Blue eyes bored into hers.

Feeling foolish, like the immature child he'd accused her of being almost three years ago, she uncovered her ears and dropped her hands out of his line of sight into her lap and curled them into fists.

With hard-won composure, Miranda said, "I'm sure being wealthy beyond belief means you've gotten used to throwing money around to make all your problems go away. But not this time. I won't take a cent."

His jaw had hardened. A shiver closely allied to fear feathered down her spine as he bit out, "Don't you think it's rather late for fine principles?"

Miranda stared at him blankly. "What do you mean?"

"You've conveniently forgotten?"

"Forgotten what?"

His lips compressed into an impatient line. "Taking money from me."

"That's a lie—I've never taken a cent from you." She'd die of starvation before she did that. He'd caused her family so much grief.

After the funeral, the house where Miranda had grown up with its apple orchard and paddocks had, by necessity, been sold along with her horse Troubadour and Adrian's expensive racing bicycles. Her mother had never gotten used to the cramped terrace house in a rundown street south of the Thames that the three of them had moved into. Even with Adrian away during the term at the exclusive boarding school Flo had refused to countenance him leaving, space was tight.

Thankfully the lump sum Ironstone Insurance had paid out after her father's death had been invested wisely, the interest paying for Adrian's and Miranda's education as well as a modest retainer to support her mother, though it left Flo only a shadow of the lifestyle she'd once taken for granted.

Yet as Miranda's gaze remained locked with Callum's, a deep sense of foreboding closed around her heart.

"So where did the funds for Greenacres come from?" he asked, naming the exclusive culinary school she'd attended. He held up two fingers. "Two years. And your brother's schooling at St. Martin's…"

No, please God.

It had been a shock to discover her parents' precarious financial position after her father's death. But at least her father had kept his life insurance up-to-date.

Voice trembling, she said, "My father's life insurance policy paid f—"

"Your father's suicide voided the policy."

"No!" She realized she was shaking her head wildly. "That can't be true."

Yet even as she denied it, her brain worked furiously. What he said sounded perfectly logical. From the stories her father had told about repudiated claims she knew about fine print. So why had the company paid out the policy after his death when they'd fired her father…had publicly branded him a criminal? And why had she never questioned the settlement?

Because she'd trusted her father not to do anything that would leave her…them…so horribly exposed. Surely he would never have killed himself, cutting them off from the last lifeline available to them?

But he had.

Why had he killed himself, and abandoned them when there'd been so much to live for? It wasn't as if he'd been guilty. Yet Thomas Owen had left his family vulnerable. And this man, a man she detested, had bailed them out.

Why?

She must have said it out loud. Because Callum shifted from one foot to the other and discomfort flashed in his eyes. Her gaze sharpened. He thought she'd been asking why he'd supported them…and that made him uncomfortable. The next *why?* popped into her head: what did Callum have to feel guilty about?

The answer hit her like a bolt of lightning, filling her with icy shock. Had it been a payoff? So they wouldn't sue Ironstone Insurance? No. Her mother would never have accepted that.

Or would she have? Miranda wavered. Things had been pretty dire after her father's death. Had her mother been tempted?

"You can't have paid for everything." *Please, please, let it not be so.*

Something like pity softened his gaze. "Do you want to see the invoices?"

Trepidation made her mouth go dry. "And the allowance my mother receives every month?" She paused. But she had to ask…had to know. "Are you paying that, too?"

His eyes told her yes.

It was too much. Miranda's stomach started to churn again. The sick feeling that had unsettled her earlier swept over her like a tidal wave.

She turned her head away and stared out the sheet-glass window over the cloud-shrouded city where the light was rapidly waning. Miranda shivered. How much had Callum paid? How much did her family owe the man responsible for her father's death? And how was she ever going to pay it back?

Just trying to figure how much money was involved made her feel all weak inside. Jerkily, she staggered to her feet and yanked her coat on, hugging its warmth around her. Slinging her bag over her shoulder, she faced him, her head held high. "I don't want this job—I don't want anything from you. And you can stop the allowance to my mother from today—she doesn't want your money, either."

She stumbled across his office. The expanse of carpet stretched forever and the door seemed a long way away.

As she grasped the doorknob, he spoke from behind her. "If I were you, I'd check that your mother feels the same way you do—you may be in for a surprise."

Two

Outside the towering glass world of Ironstone Insurance darkness had fallen. Huddled in her coat, Miranda hurried toward the bus stop. Not even the festivity of the Christmas lights twinkling through the winter gloom could lift her spirits.

A chill wind swirled around her legs as Callum's words reverberated though her head. *If I were you, I'd check that your mother feels the same way you do—you may be in for a surprise.*

Her mother couldn't have possibly known... wouldn't have hidden this from her.

Homeward-bound traffic rushed past, and Miranda fumbled in her bag for her cell phone before punching the call button with an icy, shaking finger. "Mum?"

"Hello, darling." Flo sounded cheerfully vague. "I'm home from my tea with Sorrel. What are we having for dinner?"

The mundane thought disoriented Miranda for an instant. Dinner? Who cared? She gathered her scattered thoughts together.

"I just saw Callum Ironstone. He says Dad's insurance never paid out and that Callum paid for my studies and Adrian's schooling himself." Reaching the deserted bus stop, Miranda halted and held her breath as she waited for her mother's denial.

Instead, an ominous silence. *Her mother had known.*

"Mum?"

Nothing.

"Flo—" Miranda resorted to her mother's name as she'd been doing more and more recently "—please tell me it's a lie." Unable to stand still, she took a few unsettled steps out of the shelter and paced restlessly along the sidewalk. Miranda closed her eyes, willing her mother to deny it.

"Darling…"

As her mother's breathy voice trailed away, Miranda knew Callum had told her the truth. There had never been a life insurance payout. Her gloved hands tightened round the phone and despair set in. The same evil little wind whirled around her ears, and she shivered. Opening her eyes, she glimpsed her bus trundling past the stop.

"Wait," she called, running after it.

"What did you say, darling?" Flo sounded alarmed over the open line.

"I just missed my bus." Miranda slowed to a standstill. Her next bus wasn't due for half an hour and she would be freezing by the time she got home. She wanted to howl to the dark sky. Or burst into tears. But what would that help? The phone pressed against her ear, Miranda backed up and sagged tiredly against the bus shelter, staring bleakly into the shadows.

"Darling, the Ironstones owed it to us."

"I don't want money from them." *Especially not from him.* "I want them to take responsibility for what they did to Dad." *To us.*

"This is their way of taking responsibility, by paying us money."

But it was Callum who had paid.

The chilling thought that had occurred to her in Callum's office resurfaced. Sucking the cold, damp air into her lungs, she plunged on. "Mum, was it supposed to be a payoff from the company so that we—and Dad's estate—wouldn't sue?"

"Darling, no!"

The tension that had tightened her stomach into knots eased a little. "So you didn't sign any settlement agreement?"

"There was a document," her mother admitted, "but it wasn't anything important."

"Are you sure?" Miranda prompted urgently.

"Only that I'd use the money for your and Adrian's education…and for housekeeping."

"That's all?"

"And there was a little something for me each month, too," Flo added reluctantly.

"Perhaps I should look at that agreement," said Miranda darkly.

"Oh, darling, I don't even know where it is anymore. It's nothing important. Let it go. The Ironstones took responsibility for what happened."

"Not the Ironstones. Callum Ironstone."

It had become important to make that distinction. And Miranda wished she had seen that missing agreement. She strongly suspected that Callum had rushed to the grieving widow with a contract that precluded legal action—against him, his family and their company.

And no doubt the cash had been the price of his guilty conscience. Money had freed him from what he'd done.

It made her see red.

But how could she make Flo understand she wanted Callum Ironstone to sweat blood? And his brothers, too. *And* his father, who'd been chairman at the time Miranda's father had been framed.

But more than anything it was Callum she wanted to see suffer—because he'd been her father's boss. It had been Callum who'd made the decision that had ruined her father's life. He had summarily dismissed Thomas Owen, an employee with twenty years' service to Ironstone Insurance, had him arrested, charged with a crime he hadn't committed, and then had publicly humiliated a humble, gentle man.

"Darling, Adrian says he needs a word with you."

Her mother's voice brought her back to the dark London street. Miranda shivered again. A second later her brother's voice came over the line.

"Mir?"

He sounded so young. He was the reason she'd set foot in Callum Ironstone's moneyed world today. It seemed an age since her only worry had been about what Adrian might have done. In less than an hour, Callum had turned her world upside down.

How was she ever going to find the money to pay back Callum?

"What is it?" she asked dully. The long day on her feet in The Golden Goose topped by the meeting with Callum had sapped her strength. All she craved was a warm home and a hot meal that she hadn't had to cook. And someone to hold her, to tell her that everything would be okay.

None of that would happen. She'd been cutting the heating to a minimum to save money, so the terrace house would be barely warm, and there would be no hot meal unless she cooked it herself.

Adrian interrupted her musing. "Listen, sis, I need you to lend me some money. Can you draw it out on your way home?"

"*More* money?" Only last night she'd given him fifty pounds for a night out with his friends. At least he was due to be paid on Friday. It galled her that she was actually grateful for the job he had with Ironstone Insurance, but she needed that money back. Desperately. "How much do you need this time?"

"Uh…"

A sharp edge of unease knifed her at his hesitation. Her voice rising, she asked, "How much?"

The amount made her breath catch. "Good grief, Adrian, I don't have that kind of money." Even the monthly housekeeping fund was almost empty. "What have you done?"

"Nothing, I promise you. Nothing major. I'm just helping—"

"You haven't been gambling again?"

A couple of months back Adrian had developed an addiction to blackjack, and had started frequenting casinos. His talk of developing a system that couldn't lose had struck terror into Miranda. Now images of bull-necked debt collectors threatening to break her baby brother's fingers crowded her mind. "You promised not to go back there." A promise he'd resented, but she'd insisted on it before she'd agreed to pay off his debts. "Are you in danger?"

"No!" He gave a half laugh. "I haven't been gambling. Honestly, you should hear yourself, sis—you're worse than Mum."

Flo was too soft on him. That was part of the

reason he'd gotten so close to trouble. Miranda knew it was time he grew up.

"I can't just keep giving you handouts, Adrian. You still owe me the money I lent you last ni—"

"I know, I know. You're the best sister in the world."

Miranda hesitated. "So what's this money for?"

"Oh, don't nag, sis. It's to help someone in trouble," he said cagily.

What had happened to being the best sister in the world? "Hardly nagging, given the amount you want. Can't this person find someone else to help them?"

"I've promised." Adrian sounded impatient. "It's going to be hard to back out now."

"You should've thought of that before you pledged my money."

Then wished she'd bitten her tongue when he said, "Just forget it, okay. I'll find someone else to help me—maybe I can get an advance against my pay."

And place her further in Callum's debt? Over her dead body! Miranda contemplated the amount in her savings account. Every cent she'd squirreled away for the past fourteen months. The extra jobs. The overtime. All painfully accumulated to allow her a few months of breathing space when she finally handed in her notice at The Golden Goose and started her own catering business.

It was a pittance compared to the overwhelming amount she needed to repay Callum. Her dream was already history.

She suppressed a sigh.

But at least Adrian wasn't gambling. He wasn't in trouble. Despite her fears, she hadn't been called in to Ironstone's because he'd done anything stupid. And now he'd promised to help a friend. Weren't those precisely the kind of values she'd tried to instill in him?

The time had come to start trusting his judgment; otherwise he'd never grow up.

But, oh, boy, it was hard.

"Let me see what I can do."

A pause. Then, "Thanks, sis."

"But it will be a loan, Adrian," she cautioned.

This wasn't going the way of all the other sums she'd "lent" her brother. "Your friend needs to understand that. When will I get it back?"

"Soon," he replied, with a worrying vagueness that reminded her uncomfortably of Flo. "He'll get paid—probably at the end of the next fortnight."

"I'll hold you to that." Hitting the end-call button with unaccustomed ferocity, Miranda noticed that it had started to drizzle. She shivered in the gloom. Her dream had just received a death knell, so why bother about a bit of rain?

Headlights cut through the drizzle, tires hissing as a sleek car veered toward the curb. Miranda turned away, not in the mood for unwelcome harassment.

A window lowered. "Jump in."

Callum!

Miranda hunched her shoulders and ignored him.

A door slammed, and a moment later an arm landed across her shoulders, surrounding her with warmth and comfort. Miranda was tempted to lean into his broad chest and draw the strength she could. She squared her shoulders. This was Callum Ironstone. Her enemy.

"I'm parked illegally. Let's go before I get ticketed."

She shrugged him off. "I'll wait for my bus, thanks."

He glanced up at the electronic information board above the bus shelter. "Looks like a long wait. Or would you rather freeze on principle?"

She hated that he managed to make her sound like a petulant child. Reluctantly Miranda allowed him to take her elbow—ignoring the sudden prickles of sensation—and steer her to his car, a ghost-gray Daimler. Opening the door for her, he stood back while she clambered in.

A delicious frisson rippled down her spine as the warm interior embraced her. Turning her head away as if in rejection of the seductive comfort Callum's wealth offered, Miranda stared blindly out the side window as he settled in the driver's seat beside her.

"Where to?"

The weight of Callum's gaze settled on Miranda.

"Home."

"Not The Golden Goose?"

"I've finished for the day." No point revealing what a tussle she'd had getting time off.

Instead of starting the car, he said, "I'd have thought you'd have used your qualifications to land something better than a job at a place like that."

She shrugged and stared through the windshield at traffic that had slowed to a crawl as the drizzle turned to rain. No point defending The Golden Goose. Not when what he said was true and she couldn't wait to escape.

Although any chance of that had gone up in smoke the moment he'd told her about her father's life insurance being nonexistent.

"It was the closest job I could find to home." That meant less spent on transport, less time commuting, which gave more hours to work overtime. "It's only a short bus ride away," she said tiredly. "It pays the bills."

And that was what mattered. Making sure Adrian's future education was taken care of, repaying Callum and saving enough money to look after Flo. Until she'd repaid Callum she couldn't even think of opening her own catering business.

He must have heard her sigh because he said gently, "I know your family is short of cash. You should've accepted my proposition—who knows, you might have impressed people and gotten a few more catering jobs to ease the hardship."

Did he have any idea what kind of temptation he'd dangled in front of her? How hard it had been to refuse?

She eyed him warily as he accelerated into the stream of traffic. Yes, he probably did. "Now I believe everything I've heard about you."

"Everything? You shouldn't believe everything." She caught a lightning flash of wicked blue eyes before he turned his attention back to the road. "Some rumors are nothing more than wild speculation."

Ignoring the innuendo underlying the humor,

Miranda said hastily, "That you have the ability to home in on what people want and then use it against them?" And now he was doing that to her.

Studying his profile, she took in the straight nose jutting out with masculine arrogance, quickly bypassing his generous mouth. Miranda had no idea how he'd gotten a glimpse into her soul, her deepest desire, but somehow the sneaky bastard had.

If the offer had come from anyone else…

"I'm only asking you to cater a dinner party for me. How can I use that against you?"

"I'm sure you'll find a way," she said darkly, thinking of how he'd pressured her poor mother into signing an agreement that Flo wouldn't have had a hope of understanding. No doubt it cleared the Ironstone family of all liability. Helplessness filled Miranda. How could she fight such a man?

"So why don't you prove to me that I didn't waste money putting you through cooking school?"

"Culinary school," she corrected.

"If you say so." He slowed as a light turned red. He swiveled his head, and his gaze met hers. "If it makes it easier, think of it this way. You owe it to me."

"I *owe* it to you?" The gall of the man. "I owe you nothing." *He* owed *her.* For taking her father away, for ruining her family.

Her anger and confusion trapped her. She wanted him to hurt as much as she hurt, wanted to force him to take responsibility for what he'd done. But not by making her family his pet charity. And the only thing she truly desired he could never give back.

Her father.

In the meantime, all the money Callum had given Flo had to be paid back. And once that had been accomplished, Miranda hoped the guilt of knowing what he'd done killed him.

"If you could, you'd gather what cash you could and hurl it at me right now, wouldn't you?" That rogue eyebrow quirked up again.

"Maybe," she said grudgingly, resenting the fact that he could read her so well.

He shook his head. "What a wasted effort."

"Easy for you to say."

"It will take you forever." As the lights changed, he put the car back into gear and pulled away. "You should put away your bitterness and grab this opportunity with both hands. Who knows where it could lead?"

And make a deal with this devil?

But she turned his words over in her mind. She'd already accepted it would take years to save what she owed him. And even if she did, it didn't look like his conscience would keep him awake every night of his life. Callum Ironstone probably didn't have a conscience.

So why was she tying herself into knots to pay back money he and his family wouldn't even miss? Why *not* take the bloody job?

The money was amazing. It would almost cover the amount Adrian wanted from her. Almost. If she cut corners on the household budget for the next month, she wouldn't even need to take anything from her savings.

Temptation beckoned. He'd be paying the

money to a caterer anyway. This wasn't charity. It looked perfectly straightforward.

Too perfectly straightforward.

"Why did you offer me the contract?"

"The caterer I usually use is too busy. Christmas." He gestured to the fairy lights sparkling through the rain. "And I've been too busy to hire someone else. Seeing Adrian at work this morning reminded me of you—I knew you'd have the skills. But if you don't want it, I'll find someone else."

She ought to refuse. No good would come out of this association. She even rounded her mouth to say "No."

Then she thought about Adrian, his frustration as he'd said, "Forget it." She thought about delving into her hard-earned cash to help his friend out. She *needed* the cash Callum offered.

Miranda took a deep breath and said, "Okay, I'll do it."

And when he smiled, a slow satisfied curve on his lips, Miranda hoped she hadn't made a terrible mistake.

* * *

Callum gazed across the refectory-style table at the woman he'd been fighting to ignore all evening.

Without success. Not only had Miranda cooked a meal that had made his mouth water, she'd carefully supervised the staff she'd hired, popping in and out of the dining room to check on the wine and that everything was running smoothly.

She'd even distracted him from Petra Harris, Gordon's daughter, something he'd never foreseen. Especially not tonight, of all nights.

Callum told himself it couldn't be Miranda's appearance that had him tied up in knots. Instead of a traditional white chef's jacket and herringbone trousers, she wore a plain black dress, her hair up in a knot and no glitter in sight. By rights she should've been eclipsed by every other woman in the room, and she should've looked plain and drab.

Yet she didn't.

The black only served to highlight the creamy perfection of her skin. No jewelry adorned the deliciously smooth line of her throat. And the only gold that glinted in the glow of the discreet uplighters adorning his dining room were the bits of hair that had escaped and framed her face, making her eyes look wider and more mysterious than ever.

Desire leaped within him, quickly followed by disbelief. This couldn't be happening to him.

He narrowed his eyes. This was the same girl who had once screamed at him like a banshee, accusing him of murdering her father…so why the hell couldn't he stop looking at her? He had his life—his future—all mapped out. And it didn't include Miranda Owen.

Forcing his attention back to Gordon Harris's daughter seated beside him, Callum vowed not to let himself be distracted. Hell, he'd planned to propose to Petra after dinner. In his study. Just the two of them. A quick ten-minute tête-à-tête, before announcing it in spectacular fashion to the world—he'd even invited a journalist tonight who covered the society pages. The ring box was in his pocket. Ready. Waiting. It wasn't only the merger with Gordon's company he'd planned to reveal tonight….

He gazed at the woman he'd decided would make him a perfect wife.

"The food tonight is out of this world." Petra smiled at him, revealing sparkling white teeth, and her fingers brushed his.

"I couldn't agree more." Callum tried to convince himself that powder-blue eyes were every bit as appealing as the color of melted caramel, and failed dismally. To his consternation, there was no spark of electrical charge from the brush of her fingers, either.

"Would you like crème caramel or strawberry cheesecake?" Miranda asked.

Adrenaline surged through him. He could've sworn he'd sensed Miranda's approach even before she spoke beside him, and every nerve went on red alert as he picked up the subtle scent of vanilla. Her innocent offer of dessert made him instantly desire far more carnal pleasures. Damn, what the hell was happening?

"Strawberry cheesecake for me," said Petra,

giving Miranda an easy smile. "I was just complimenting Callum on the fabulous spread tonight."

"Thank you." A flush of pleasure lit Miranda's cheeks, making her look even more downright sexy. "May I suggest a Sauterne or ice wine to accompany it?"

"Ooh, I'll have ice wine. Sounds delicious."

"I'll bring you a clean glass." Miranda stretched past Callum to remove Petra's wineglass. The tension within him twisted higher as she brushed against him. When she reached forward, the black fabric of her dress tightened across the gentle valley of her belly, accentuating the feminine indent of her waist and the rounded curve of her hip. He couldn't tear his gaze away.

She straightened. "What would you like?"

What would he like?

Thank God she couldn't read his mind. She'd run a mile. He glanced up and connected with the melting eyes that so entranced him. Prosaically, she repeated the choices.

"Crème caramel, please," he muttered, his

throat suddenly thick as a mental image of himself offering her a spoonful of the rich dessert flashed through his mind. He visualized her pink tongue delicately licking the creamy texture off the spoon, her lashes flicking up. Her eyes, glowing and golden, promising him untold delights and—

"That's all?"

"All?" he croaked, then realized his eyes were raking her body, so he jerked his attention away.

It wasn't all; he wanted so much more…

God, this was stupid! And the sparks had been sizzling ever since she had arrived earlier in the evening. He'd found himself hanging around the kitchen—he'd offered her a glass of Merlot to give himself an excuse to watch her—until the arrival of the two women he'd hired to serve his guests had sent him scuttling for his study and a shot of whiskey.

He'd been grateful when his half brothers, Jack and Hunter, had arrived with their dinner partners so that he could escape her thrall. Gordon and Petra had come soon after.

There was nothing special about Miranda. She wasn't nearly as beautiful as Petra—and she was extremely prickly and difficult—yet she intrigued him.

When last had he experienced anything like this?

Guilt ate at him. He was conscious of the ring he'd chosen lying heavy in his pocket. How the hell was he supposed to propose to Petra when his headspace was full of Miranda?

He glanced around the table, claustrophobia closing in on him. His brother, Fraser, gave him a grin.

This was his coup—he'd organized every last detail. There'd always been healthy competition between him and his brother, Fraser, and his two half brothers. Being the youngest of the four, he'd been last to make it onto the board of the company. But he'd intended to be the first to marry.

Yet now that the time had come to propose to Petra…he couldn't. Instead he wanted to bolt.

Perhaps this inexplicable crazy lust for

Miranda was nothing more than a flight response to his carefully planned siege of Petra.

He drew a gulp of air in relief. Fear. That's what this was. It wasn't about Miranda at all—she was simply a convenient excuse.

He gave Petra an uncomfortable smile. "Enjoying yourself?"

Her father leaned forward. "We all are."

A chorus of agreement followed.

"Such a pity the snowed-up roads prevented your parents from joining us."

Callum seized on his parents' absence. How could he announce his engagement without them present? They'd never forgive him. He scanned the faces around the table. Everyone *was* having a fantastic time—except for him.

Under Petra's smile, he shifted. He knew Gordon had great expectations for this relationship with Petra. Callum hadn't slept with her yet, though both he and Petra had known they were headed for the bedroom; he'd wanted the contracts signed…and a ring on her finger first.

He stuck one hand into his jacket pocket.

"Crème caramel," Miranda announced.

Just her husky tone was enough to make him start at the want that resurged. Taking his hand out of his pocket, he stared at the dessert she'd placed on the starched white-damask tablecloth in front of him. Creamy custard…and caramelized sugar the same rich golden brown as her eyes.

He picked up a spoon.

The dessert was smooth on his tongue. Sweet and silky. With a hint of vanilla. The caramel rich and tangy.

Would Miranda taste as delectable?

Hell! And he was getting hard just thinking about it. Callum shifted uncomfortably and forced himself to focus on the dinner conversation.

In the kitchen, Miranda rested her head against the cool, hand-painted Italian tiles and suppressed the urge to swear violently.

"Are you okay?" Jane, one of the women Callum had hired to help tonight, touched her shoulder lightly.

Miranda straightened. "I'm fine."

But she wasn't. Something had happened out there in the dining room—something she didn't understand. Callum had looked at her, and she had responded like a sunflower greeting the morning sun. And the realization pierced her heart like a shard of ice.

Please, not him.

She hated him.

Miranda reached with a shaky hand for what was left of the glass of red wine Callum had poured her earlier, and drained it. Jane picked up a bottle and silently topped her glass.

"Thanks." Miranda smiled at the other woman. "Believe it or not, I never drink when I'm working."

"It's a good vintage." Jane helped herself to a wineglass out the cupboard. After filling the glass she lifted it. "Very nice."

Miranda felt a rush of gratitude. "Thank you." She took a sip and set the glass down. "I'm okay now. Let's get on with the coffees."

By the time she went out into the dining room, she told herself she had her reactions in check. The wine had warmed her, dissolving the icy chill. As she passed the end of the long dining table, an older man asked her for a card and Miranda flushed when she realized she didn't have any. Something she would remedy tomorrow.

Moving up the table, she was breathlessly aware of Callum's dark, brooding presence at the head. Given that he looked devilishly good in a black dinner jacket with a pristine white shirt, keeping her resolve was far from easy.

She smiled at the woman sitting beside him who had complimented her cooking, and tried to ignore the way the woman's fingers brushed Callum's dinner-jacketed arm when she made a point.

After one searing look from Callum, Miranda averted her gaze, and turned away, making sure to busy herself down at the other end of the table.

This powerful awareness of Callum was a complication she didn't need.

Thank God dinner was over.

After the planning he'd put into the evening,

the end was an anticlimax. Callum could hardly wait to see Petra, her father and his family out the front door. The confusion in Petra's expectant eyes made him feel like an utter bastard.

"I'll talk to you tomorrow," he said, ushering her off behind her father.

Talk to her? And say what? How in heaven's name was he supposed to explain something he didn't even understand himself?

He justified that it could've been worse. What if he'd already been engaged to Petra when this urge to chase Miranda like a hound after a bitch in heat had taken hold? It made him go stone-cold.

This second-thoughts stuff must be normal. Wedding-ring fright. But he wouldn't run away. He'd deal with it the same way he did every other problem he met: head-on. Confront this inconvenient lust, the need to indulge in one last chase. Get Miranda out his system. Then marry Petra exactly as he'd planned.

Simple.

Closing the door behind the last of his guests, Callum went to find Miranda. Anticipation lent lightness to his step. He peered into the library—his favorite haunt—but it was empty. Not that he'd expected to discover her there.

He finally tracked her down in the scullery tucked away at the far end of the kitchen. Miranda was busy stacking the dirty dishes into the drawers of the state-of-the-art dishwasher.

She'd donned an apron, an absurd white bit of cotton with a ruffle along the hem below a bib that barely covered her front. It lent the black dress she wore the naughty severity of a French maid costume.

Callum breathed deeply. "What are you doing?"

She kept her eyes down. "Cleaning up."

Given the boiling heat that simmered in him, her lack of interest irritated. He marched forward and said more stridently than he intended, "Where's the help I hired?"

"The *help* you hired?" She straightened, affront glittering in her eyes. "They have names. Emily and Jane. They're people. Emily was tired—she's been up since dawn and she has a long way to go to get home."

"So where's the other one?"

One finely arched eyebrow rose. "You mean Jane?"

He nodded impatiently. "Yes, Jane."

"Her brother picked her up."

"And even though you've been at work preparing food long before they arrived, they left you with all the mess?"

"They cleared most of it." She gestured to the adjoining kitchen. "And the leftover food has been itemized and frozen. I'm just packing in the coffee cups and dessert dishes, Emily and Jane—" she used their names pointedly "—have already run the dishwasher twice, and unpacked it."

She strode past him into the kitchen and looked around. "All nice and tidy, see?"

Callum followed and leaned back against the center island. Folding his arms across his chest, he said, "And what about you? Don't you have to hurry home?"

"Of course." She stalked across to a row of hooks and picked off her bag and a black woolen coat. Dropping the bag and coat on the center island, she unzipped a side pocket and retrieved her cell phone. "But I've been paid an astronomical amount for tonight's dinner—I'm making sure you get your money's worth."

His money's worth?

The words taunted, especially from a woman wearing such a starkly erotic outfit. With an effort he focused his attention back on her face. "It's what I always pay."

Her eyes went round. He could see her thoughts buzzing as she calculated. "And you entertain often?"

"Yes, but it's work." As well as being part of the rationale for courting Petra. He needed a wife.

And Petra would be perfect.

He only needed to propose….

Yet he couldn't imagine Petra looking so innocently erotic in the black-and-white getup that Miranda was wearing. Or having this

effect on him. His erection throbbed painfully
behind the concealing fabric of his pants.

Callum shut his eyes.

And opened them to find Miranda staring at
him. The silence in the kitchen pounded in his
ears. Her mouth was lush, her eyes meltingly seductive. Driven by an urge he couldn't resist, he
took a step forward.

His hands settled on her upper arms, the flesh
soft and giving under his fingers. Hoarsely, he
asked, "I've been wanting to taste you all night.
Are you as sweet as the crème caramel?"

Callum gave her a moment to object. Time
stopped. She didn't move. Or say anything. His
hands slid around her and he pulled her to him.
The warm scent of vanilla enfolded him, so
feminine, so seductive.

He took the phone out of her unresisting hand
and set it down on the island.

Her lips remained closed as he kissed her, not
accepting, but not rejecting him, either.

Callum raised his head, and looked down into
her face. There was a startled awareness in her

eyes. His mouth slanted as he said, "Not as sweet as I'd expected."

She started to say something, and in a flash he bent his head and took advantage of her parted lips.

His tongue sank in, and he plundered the warm, private cave. He'd lied. She tasted sweeter than sin. Of rich red wine, spicy cinnamon and seductive woman.

When her tongue swirled around his, Callum gave a moan of satisfaction.

Instantly Miranda's body softened against his, melting into him. Heat swept over him. His hands pressed into the small of her back, drawing her against the blatant evidence of his arousal.

She didn't pull away as he'd half expected.

His fingers played with the bow that fastened her apron behind her back and it came loose. "Do you know how sexy this outfit is?" he murmured against her mouth.

"An apron is sexy?"

"Oh, God…*yes.*"

She laughed, a lilting sound that drove him

wild. He put his mouth over hers, tasting the musical notes. Ah, but she was delicious.

Her hands came up between them and pushed against his chest. "I shouldn't be doing this."

Callum let her back away. "Why not?"

"Because."

He started to smile. "Because why?"

"You're going to make me say it, aren't you?"

His smile faded and he tensed, bracing himself for the accusations, ready to argue that actions had consequences, that wrongdoing couldn't escape unpunished, that she had to let it go.

Her eyes warred with his. "I don't like you."

Relief surged through him. They weren't about to discuss the circumstances of her father's death while desire raged through him and blood pounded in his head. He wanted her back in his arms. It was insane. "Liking me has nothing to do with *this*."

He whirled Miranda round and pinned her against the island, his thigh between hers. Miranda gasped at the pressure against a sensitive area, her fingers digging into his upper arms.

This time Callum gave no quarter, kissing her until they were both breathless. By the time he'd finished, she was clinging to him.

"You love that, don't you?" Some demon within him demanded a concession from her.

But she remained mute, her eyes sparkling with defiance, her cheeks flushed with high wild color.

He hoisted her up onto the silver countertop, ignoring her squawk of protest. One of her pumps clattered to the tiled floor.

"My shoe."

"Never mind your shoe." He stepped between her parted thighs, forcing her dress's hemline higher, and bending his head he placed open-mouthed kisses against the too-tempting smooth skin of her neck.

Her head lolled back, granting him unrestricted access. Lower down his hands ran along her nylon-clad thighs, he ruched her dress up farther, and when she didn't stop him, Callum moved in for the kill.

Stroking her thigh, his fingers encountered a lacy stocking edge…then soft, satiny bare skin. He groaned as he realized she wasn't wearing panty hose.

"Grief, woman, you know how to fuel a man's fantasies," he growled close to her ear as he caressed the tender flesh of her inner thigh.

Miranda only moaned, her hands knotting in his shirt.

Callum was past coherent thought. He stripped off first his dinner jacket, then ripping the snaps of his dinner shirt apart, let it fall on the stainless steel slab behind her.

"Oh."

The sound of wonder that escaped her as she gazed boldly at his bare chest made him feel like a god. He cupped her face in his hands and kissed her mouth with slow, deliberate intent, outlining the shape with the tip of his tongue. Miranda responded with hunger, and what had started out as a leisurely kiss erupted into no-holds-barred ardor.

Callum ran his hands under the loosened apron, over breasts and stomach still covered by her dress, down along her legs. He paused to caress the hollows behind her stockinged knees, then retraced the path to where the nylons ended.

After hesitating only a moment, he let his fingers drift higher until he encountered silky panties. His fingertips slid under the edge and slipped into her moist heat.

She arched against his hand. His fingers delved deeper. Her hips rocked invitingly. He buried his head in the valley between her breasts and tongued the soft hollow. Her fingers dug into his hair and pulled him closer. A roaring hunger surged through him.

This could only end one way.

With his free hand, Callum reached for his belt and zipper.

"So sweet."

He shoved down his trousers and briefs with impatient hands, then eased her closer, her thighs splayed around his hips.

The stainless steel was shockingly cold and hard. "You must be freezing."

She shook her head, arched back…and shivered. "Wait."

He stilled at her command. Disappointment, hot and sharp as a blade, twisted in his gut. Slowly, with aching regret, he withdrew his hand from her warmth. "Why are you stopping?"

Bewilderment made him raise his head. It changed when he saw the foil package that lay in the palm of her hand, her open bag upended on the bench. God. He hadn't even thought about a condom. But she'd had the presence of mind to protect them both.

He took it, tore it open and sheathed himself. "Are you sure, Miranda?"

She nodded, and her arms reached for him.

Euphoria filled him. Callum grabbed his shirt, bunched it up in a fist, and wedged it gently in behind her to pad her from the counter edge.

Then, unable to restrain himself another second, he positioned himself and pushed forward into the woman who'd been driving him wild all night.

Three

Miranda opened her eyes, caught one glimpse of the naked male torso she was snuggled up to, and a wave of mortification crashed over her.

Callum.

Oh, no! What had she done?

She lay rigid, not daring to breathe. Thankfully the man she'd fallen so foolishly into bed with last night was still asleep. Miranda suppressed a groan. And after that impulsive coupling up against the kitchen counter, she'd let him carry her upstairs—and make love to her all over again.

Let him? If anything she'd been a willing, totally wanton participant. It made her feel sick with guilt.

She cracked her eyes open and caught a glimpse of the dark mahogany bedhead. Beyond, pale winter-morning light spilled through sash windows into the bedroom. *His* bedroom.

Soon he'd waken. The idea of him finding her naked in his bed filled her with horror. Taking a deep breath, she inched her leg toward the edge of the bed. He stirred. Miranda froze.

After long, dragging seconds she slowly relaxed. He hadn't woken. Shifting her weight to the edge of the mattress, she was conscious of her heartbeat drumming loudly in her chest.

An arm slid over her, and a large male hand closed familiarly over the top of her breast. Miranda forced herself to keep absolutely still.

Oh, help!

What to do now?

Her first impulse to push that possessive hand away and leap out of his bed receded as the strong male fingers stilled.

Affront mixed with adrenaline. He'd gone back to sleep!

Eyes darting to and fro, Miranda formulated a plan. Her dress and knickers lay in a pile on the floor. Her shoes were nowhere in sight—probably scattered across the kitchen floor. She shuddered at the memories that evoked.

How could she have done such things with this man?

She blocked it all out and turned her mind back to what dominated her now: escape.

If she rolled out of bed, she could scoop up her clothes and make a run for it. With luck she'd be out the bedroom door before he'd wake and realize she'd gone. Downstairs she'd grab her shoes, her coat and her bag—which should be on the bench top where she'd left it the evening before. An image of the contents—emergency condoms, lipstick, hairbrush, wallet, cell phone—scattered over the countertop flashed through her mind and she groaned silently.

Cell phone, she thought. Her breath caught. Her mother!

She never stayed out all night. Flo would be worried sick, had probably left a dozen anxious messages.

But at least she'd be able to come out of this disastrous encounter knowing she couldn't be pregnant—or worse. Although right now that seemed small compensation for last night's stupidity.

Miranda hauled in a shallow breath and readied herself to flee.

"So you're still alive?" Provocative fingers explored the rise of her hip. "For a moment I thought you'd given up breathing—that you might require a little mouth-to-mouth resuscitation."

Callum's lazy confidence cast despair into Miranda. He'd probably been awake from the start. There'd never been any chance of a hasty getaway. Bastard.

She curled into a tight ball, refusing to acknowledge him.

"Come now." He tightened his hold, rolling her over onto her back. Wide-awake blue eyes stared down into hers. "It was better than that—in fact it was bloody fantastic…for both of us." Satisfaction oozed from that throaty growl.

Miranda careened between wishing she could actually expire from humiliation and a fierce urge to murder the naked man beside her.

Conceited ape!

Well, there was only one way to get out of this situation—and that was with what little dignity she could muster.

She sat up, making sure she took a large swath of the sheet with her to keep her breasts covered and tossed her hair back. "Don't flatter yourself. It wasn't *that* good."

His eyes ignited with laughter. "You've forgotten so soon? My sweet, you were *begging*."

A flush of heat stained her cheeks, then spread across her entire body. Damn. She couldn't deny it. But he was despicable.

Since when had she ever harbored any illusions about Callum Ironstone? She constrained herself to a look of disdainful dislike.

Under the sheet his hand came to life, playing

knowingly over her all-too-responsive flesh as it edged onto the swell of her breast.

"Stop it." Her arm lashed out, knocking the offending hand away, and with horror she realized the sheet had fallen, too.

"Nice." His eyes turned molten. His hand came up and he stroked the underside of her breasts. "Delectable, in fact." Her nipples had peaked at his touch and now ached with piercing tingles of desire.

Delectable? A fresh wave of heat flooded her. Followed quickly by anger.

How could she have responded with such lack of inhibition to this man?

"Get out of my way." She leaped from the bed, and, taking time only to snag up her clothes, she bolted for the en suite where she locked the door and started to dress with frantic haste.

After pulling on jeans, Callum galloped down the stairs and got into the kitchen just in time to see Miranda shoveling her things off the countertop into her bag.

From behind her, his eyes lingered on the strands of gold that glowed like dancing sunbeams in the morning light and he resisted the urge to pull her into his arms, kiss her and tousle the waves into a more bedded look. Somehow he didn't think she'd appreciate passion right now.

She pushed a hairbrush into her bag with a hasty movement.

He took a step toward her unable to resist the impulse to say, "At least be honest and admit you loved every moment of last night."

She started at the sound of his voice. Her head jerked around and he saw her eyes held the look of a trapped deer. "I only did it because I owe you. Remember?"

His mind blanked out. "Because you owe me?"

"Money." She backed up but rubbed her forefinger and thumb together with bravado, her expression defiant. "For putting me through culinary school."

"Last night was payback?"

"Uh-huh." She nodded and her hair bobbed around her face.

"You slept with me because you felt indebted?" Outrage swamped Callum. No woman had *ever* slept with him to prostitute herself. What had been an amazing experience suddenly felt sordid. Annoyed, he said, "I paid a fortune. One night wouldn't begin to cover my outlay."

Her shoulders stiffened. Instead of replying, Miranda turned her back on him and gathered the last few of her scattered belongings together before dropping them into her bag. She zipped it shut with a decisive movement.

She was leaving, Callum realized.

The rigid line of her back spelt out her intention to put as much distance between them as she could. She shoved his jacket aside with unnecessary force.

"Hey, that's my favorite Armani."

His attempt to lighten the mood fell flat. The jacket slithered over the edge and, despite her grab for it, fell to the ground.

"Sorry." She bent to pick it up and Callum heard his car keys jingle as they slid from the pocket. "What's this?"

Her eyes, shockingly close, were on the same level as his as he knelt, too. For a moment he felt as if he'd been sucked into her soft, melting center.

"What's what?" he asked huskily, unable to tear his gaze away.

"This…"

He glanced down at the dark blue velvet ring box lying in the palm of her hand.

Crap.

"It's a jeweler's box." She stated the obvious before he could reply. Already her fingers were working the catch.

Alarm electrified him. "No. Don't."

Too late.

For long seconds Miranda stared at the diamond solitaire ring inside. Then she raised eyes full of questions. "You planned to ask me to marry you?"

Callum had the disoriented sense that he'd just been catapulted into an alien world. He couldn't think. Hell, he couldn't breathe—his lungs were empty.

"Why?" Her eyes held a luminosity that twisted his gut into knots.

"Uh…" He gulped in air.

"Because you slept with me?" A puzzled frown furrowed her brow as she lifted the ring from the bed of velvet and caressed it with her fingertips. "No. That's not right. You had the ring before you slept with me. So…"

This was not going as he'd planned. He could see her thinking, coming to the Lord knew what conclusion.

Ah, hell. "Not you," he muttered.

"What?" Her full attention zeroed in on him again.

"I wasn't going to propose to you."

An indecipherable expression flashed across her face. "Then who?"

He saw the moment she put it together. Her eyes went dark and blank. "Petra."

He nodded slowly, uneasy at the way Miranda was looking at him.

"You asked Petra to marry you last night." She dropped the ring back into the box and the lid snapped shut, the sound loud in the early morning silence. Then she stood up and he heard the box skip across the stainless steel bench.

He flinched. Miranda thought—

"Hang on," he said urgently, leaping to his feet.

But she ignored him. Swinging on her heel, she marched across the kitchen, her heels tap-tapping a furious tattoo on the matte wooden floor.

"Hey, you don't understand." He reached out to restrain her as she stomped past.

She turned her head and gave him a contemptuous glare. His hand fell away.

"Oh, I understand too well. You asked the daughter of a new major shareholder to marry you. She had the sense to refuse, so you slept with the hired help—" she spat out the last two words "—in a fit of pique." She punctuated her conclusion by marching to the door into the house and slamming it behind her.

A click followed.

Callum skidded after her, only to find she'd locked the door from the hall side. By the time he'd rushed out the back door, through the mews, and around to the front of the row of town houses, Miranda was gone.

The beastly two-timing jerk.

Miranda was still fuming when she arrived at The Golden Goose shortly before noon on Sunday. Fortunately Flo had accepted her arrival home in the clothes she'd gone out in last night with no questions, glossing over Miranda's stuttered excuse about working late.

Her mother's skirting the issue hadn't soothed her as much as it should've. Nor did it help that Gianni, the longtime chef, was glowering at her over the chopping block while Mick, the manager, danced around muttering that she was late—even though Miranda knew she'd walked in the door at five minutes to midday.

The final straw came when Mick cornered her later to say that her commitment was lacking. She'd left early last week, and now she was late and she was to take this as a warning. In these tough times, he expected more.

Gianni gave her a sly grin as she passed him, confirming where the heart of the problem lay. She wished she could reassure him, tell him that she had no ambitions to take over his job. But she knew that would only make him rush to tell Mick about her lack of commitment.

She was screwed.

By the time she got home late that night, Miranda was ill-prepared for the sight of an ostentatious bunch of long-stemmed pink roses that must've cost some joker a fortune.

And she suspected she knew who the joker might be.

"An admirer from last night?" Flo arched a finely penciled eyebrow. "I thought you said it was work."

"Must be a thank-you," Miranda bit out, ripping off the still-sealed envelope and pocketing it to get it out of her mother's line of sight.

"So considerate." Flo touched the blooms with reverent fingers. "They're beautiful. I watered them. Why don't you put them in your bedroom?"

And be stuck looking at a reminder of last

night's calamity? No, thanks! Stalking away, Miranda wished she hadn't said they were a thank-you; now she couldn't even throw the wretched flowers away.

"Someone rang for you earlier."

Miranda froze in the doorway, but didn't turn around. "Who?"

"A man. He had a rough voice. It was strangely familiar," said Flo slowly.

Miranda stifled an anxious groan. "Did he leave a name?" She prayed not. Her mother didn't need to know she'd been fraternizing with the Ironstones.

"No. He said he'd catch you on your cell phone."

Her cell phone had been off while she worked. "Thanks, Mum."

After setting down the unopened white envelope on the dressing table in her room, Miranda made for the bathroom the three of them shared. After she'd showered the odors of The Golden Goose away, she changed into a flannel nightie and brushed her teeth.

Climbing into bed, she finally picked up her

cell phone and switched it on. The message light flashed. She stared at it for long seconds.

No. She had no intention of giving in to curiosity and checking to see if Callum had left her a message. The man had dominated her thoughts far too much already. And she was not about to let him cause her another sleepless night.

Setting the phone on the bed stand, she turned the lamp off, refusing to let herself dwell on the reason why she'd slept so little last night....

Four

Miranda was wakened the following morning by banging on her bedroom door. She'd barely opened her eyes before Adrian barged in.

"Phone." He held out the handset. "Callum."

Her heart sank. She wished fervently she hadn't been too cowardly to check her cell phone the night before. Now she was at a decided disadvantage. "Thanks."

Adrian hovered in the doorway, clearly curious. But an older-sister scowl caused him to roll his eyes and depart. When his footfalls finally faded, she lifted the handset to her ear. "Yes?"

"What happened to good morning?" Callum sounded delighted.

She squinted at her bedside clock. "Do you have any idea what time it is?"

"Although now that I think about it, you didn't greet me yesterday, either. Maybe you're not a morning person."

He had that right. But nor did she want any reminder about waking in his bed yesterday morning. "What do you want?"

"Now there's a leading question." He'd lowered his voice to a husky drawl and at once a rush of heat filled Miranda. Oh, heavens! She couldn't let herself respond to Callum with such unfettered sensual delight.

She tamped it down. "Oh, please, it's too early in the morning for sexual innuendo."

He laughed. "Definitely not a morning person. I apologize for calling so early." That must be a first. "I'm flying out to New York this afternoon," Callum continued more briskly, "and my schedule this morning is hellish."

Miranda suppressed the urge to cheer at the thought of Callum over three thousand miles away—it would give her time to recover from the turmoil that sleeping with him had caused her.

He was still talking rapidly. "I've got tickets for *Les Misérables* on Saturday night. Do you want to go? We can have dinner afterward."

"You called me to invite me on a *date?*" she said, blank dismay settling over her.

The silence stretched. Then he said, "I suppose you could call it that."

What else did one call a show and dinner followed by whatever else he had in mind? Shivers prickled as vivid images of what he might be planning assailed her.

The last thing she needed was an affair with Callum Ironstone. She already despised herself enough for allowing him to seduce her— although to be fair she'd been more than willing. If she hadn't had those glasses of red wine…if he hadn't been so damn tempting…if he hadn't kissed her and turned her legs to jelly.

Oh, God, she couldn't believe she was letting herself relive it all. Callum had taken her to bed the same night he'd proposed to another woman. Because of him her father was dead. How could she have let him touch her? Seeing him again would be a betrayal of her very soul.

"No, I can't come."

"Another evening then?"

"No." She hung up.

The phone rang again. She glared at it. Then picked it up before Adrian—or Flo—could.

"Did you get the message I left on your cell phone last night?"

"No," she said guardedly, eyeing the phone that winked a message on the bedside table. "But whatever you said wouldn't have changed my answer."

"You believe I only slept with you because Petra rejected me."

That was only the tip of the iceberg. She was furious with herself for sleeping with him at all. Furious with him for making it so easy. "Yes? So what?"

"I never asked Petra to marry me," he said.

"You didn't?"

"That's the message I left for you yesterday."

"Oh." She fell silent. Why had he told her this? She wouldn't allow it to be important. Yet her pulse quickened. Miranda drew a steadying breath, aware that she had to tread carefully.

"It doesn't make any difference, Callum." She couldn't afford to alienate him. He'd given Adrian a vacation job, which might lead to a permanent placement next year. If she annoyed Callum, he might fire Adrian. "I just don't think it's a good idea for me to date you."

She heard him whisper "Liar" just as she hurriedly severed the connection.

This time he didn't ring back. But before she could set foot out of bed, Adrian slipped into her room.

"What did Callum want?"

She wasn't telling him that his boss, her

nemesis, had asked her on a date. "Nothing to do with you."

Adrian looked sick. "Sis, please be nice to him."

Adrian's anxiety reinforced her own worry that if she annoyed Callum he'd take it out on her brother. But there was a limit to how far she'd go—and Adrian had to know that.

"Be nice?" She loaded the meaning. "What are you asking me to do here, Adrian?"

"I mean be polite." His Adam's apple bobbed. "Nothing more. I don't want to lose this opportunity to get a good reference."

She hated the idea that Adrian thought she'd jeopardize his work. Was that how bitter she'd become?

Miranda crossed her fingers under the bedclothes. "I did some catering for Callum. We were talking about that."

His expression cleared. "That's great. So you'll be doing more work for him?"

"I didn't say that," she said hastily.

"I told him you were a good chef—that you were wasted at The Golden Goose."

"The Goose is convenient." Miranda fixed her brother with a narrow stare. Adrian must have told Callum about her dream to run her own catering business. At least that meant her fear that Callum had been able to read her like an open book had been…relatively baseless. "What else did you tell him?"

Her brother spread his hands. "Nothing. I swear."

She studied him as she swung her legs out of bed. "Okay, I believe you. Now scoot—I want to get dressed."

But he lingered. "Uh…when will you give me that money?"

"I'll go to the bank today."

"Sis…" He hesitated, then said in a rush, "Can you add another couple hundred quid?"

She paused in front of the wardrobe. "*More* money? When you still haven't repaid me the fifty pounds I lent you last week?"

He all but ran out of her room. "We can talk about it when you're dressed," he said over his shoulder.

Adrian had made breakfast by the time she got to the kitchen. Miranda drew out one of the pine chairs that Flo had sewed yellow-and-white-checked gingham covers for and stared suspiciously at the spread on the table. Scrambled eggs. Bacon. Mushrooms. Toast. Marmalade. Her favorites. "Is this a bribe?"

"No." But he looked sufficiently guilty for her to frown at him. "I took Mum her food on a tray."

"So now it's just you and me." Miranda sighed as she sat down. "Okay, explain to me why I should pay another cent to sort out your friend's problems. Hasn't he got family of his own?"

Adrian turned a dull red that clashed with his freckles. "It's not for a friend. It's for me."

"A new pair of shoes?" she asked snippily. "You know I'm saving. Can't this wait?"

"No." He looked down at his plate for long seconds. When he looked up, Miranda was shocked at the desperation in his expression. "I'm in trouble."

All her worst fears crowded in. "Tell me."

"Last Monday night—"

"When you went out with your friends?"

He nodded. "I borrowed a car from work, but I crashed it—hit a concrete pillar in a basement parking lot as we were leaving a club."

Horror filled her. "Everyone was okay?" The pounding of her heart slowed at his nod, and relief seeped through her, turning her limbs weak. No one had been hurt...or worse. "Were you drunk?"

"No." He looked shaken. "I never drink and drive."

She relaxed enough to fork a mouthful of food into her mouth. "So get the car fixed."

"I've already had it repaired—and borrowed money from my friends to pay for it. But the amount was more than the original quote—that's why I need more money. And they're pressing me to repay them."

I don't have any more money. Not for this. Miranda bit back her wail of despair, as the extent of his deceit struck her. "You lied to me."

"I didn't want you to know." Even his neck was red now. "I'm sorry."

She restrained herself from asking what else he'd held back from her, and pondered on the fix he was in. "Wait, you shouldn't be paying— the car belongs to Ironstone. It will be insured. Just fill out an incident report and let Ironstone handle the claim."

"I can't." He looked utterly wretched. "I wasn't supposed to have the car out after work hours. There might be criminal charges for theft if anyone at Ironstone finds out."

"Theft?" She stared at him in alarm.

"Yes, for taking the car without the owner's consent." He suddenly looked very young, re-minding her that he'd only recently finished school and was little more than a schoolboy. "I'm really sorry, sis."

Miranda knew exactly how Callum would react if he found out—and being sorry wouldn't help. He'd have Adrian arrested, and prosecute him to the full extent of the law. Look what he'd done to their father.

She couldn't let that happen again.

"I'll get you the money today." She thought

with regret about the fantasy of her own catering business, then dismissed it. Adrian was more important.

But maybe if she explained it all to Callum he might understand. There was a chance. Today was her day off, and Callum had said he was flying out this afternoon.

If she hurried she could see him before he left.

"It won't happen again." Adrian's promise got her attention.

"Better not," she growled. "Now eat your breakfast."

"I'm not hungry." He pushed back his chair and picked up the plate, crossing to the sink. "I'm going to work."

This time Miranda arrived at the Ironstone Insurance building without the benefit of being expected, and the receptionist wasn't nearly as friendly.

"Mr. Ironstone is busy," she said.

"I only need five minutes." Miranda had to

speak to Callum before he left for New York. Had to make him see that Adrian was a good boy, that he'd made a mistake in taking the car—and that all the damage would be paid for.

Because the alternative was unthinkable. Prison. She couldn't let this ruin her brother's life. Miranda shuddered as memories plagued her. Her father had been arrested…and then he'd been dead. So final. It wasn't going to happen to Adrian.

"Mr. Ironstone is not available."

"I know, Callum's going to New York—he told me. I presume he's in that meeting," she tacked on, trying to sound as though she was privy to his every plan.

The receptionist shot an indecisive look in the direction of a closed door leading off the reception area before turning her attention back and giving Miranda a curious look.

Just then the door cracked open. "Biddy, can you make four copies of this report, please?"

The receptionist came round the counter, and Miranda saw her chance. "Callum," she called out.

He looked up, and his eyes crinkled into a smile. "Miranda, what are you doing here?"

"I have to talk to you. In private," she added urgently as she glanced past him into the occupied boardroom.

"I'll be with you in a minute." He rapidly made excuses to his board members and ushered her along the corridor into his office.

"You've changed your mind?" he asked, closing the door. His eyes were warmer than she'd ever imagined the color blue could be.

Changed her mind? She blinked at him as she settled into the soft sofa beneath the bookshelves. Oh, the date! He thought she was here because she'd decided to accept?

"No—"

Help. He was moving closer, seating himself beside her. The heat that she'd sworn she would not allow herself to feel swamped her anew. His fingers closed on her upper arms. For a moment she was so incredibly tempted just to give in, to let him kiss her. But she couldn't.

"Uh…I wanted to talk about…"

He bent his head. That smiling mouth held her entranced. In a second it would land on hers.

"No!" She ducked away to the far end of the sofa. "You can't kiss me. You're going to marry Petra." She gabbled the first thing that came into her head.

He blinked. "I am?"

"You bought her a ring." He must've spent a fortune on it. That meant he had to be serious.

The powerful surge of adrenaline ebbed, and her brains unscrambled. Petra's father was an important figure in his life now that Gordon Harris held so much stock in Ironstone. That's why men like Callum married.

Not for love. Or even desire.

But for cold, sound financial reasons.

And Petra would accept with alacrity. Callum was a catch. An Ironstone. Not everyone held the view of him Miranda did.

In her mind she replayed that disaster on Saturday night when she'd ended up sprawled over his kitchen counter, and later in his bed. All evening she'd been conscious of his gaze following her, setting her body aflame. Even while he'd listened to Petra, talked to her father, been ribbed by his brothers…the whole time he'd been watching her.

All his brothers had been there. To meet Gordon, he'd told her here in this very office. A celebration.

Celebration…

Of what? She'd thought he'd been referring to the merger. Had it been something else entirely?

"Those two guests you told me couldn't make it because of the snowstorm up north. They were your parents, weren't they?"

"Well…yes."

Her suspicions crystallized into certainty. "You were going to announce your engagement."

The utter silence told Miranda she was right.

"But you didn't announce it…because you didn't get around to proposing to her," she said, following her line of thought through to the natural conclusion. "And you slept with me instead." Miranda tilted her head. "Have you broken up with her?"

He stretched. "Miranda—"

Callum hadn't broken off whatever relationship he had going with Petra. For some reason he'd simply decided he wanted *her.*

"Miranda, wait—"

He was despicable. She shifted farther into the corner of the couch. "Yes or no?"

He shook his head.

The phone on the highly polished desk rang twice before stopping abruptly. Callum glared across at it, then back to her. "The meeting is ready to continue. I have to go." But he didn't rise. "If you change your mind, call me."

"I won't," she stated with absolute conviction. "And don't invite me out again. Call Petra—she's still the woman you plan to marry."

There was no doubt in her mind that Petra would accept him.

Poor thing.

"If you say so." His eyes cooled further. "So why did you come?" His hard mouth bore no trace of a smile.

She hesitated, aware of the chasm that yawned between them, much wider than the distance that separated them on the sofa. Adrian had asked her to be nice. This didn't look like a man who would give her—or Adrian—the benefit of the doubt.

But she had to try. "How's Adrian getting—" She broke off.

"Adrian? Getting along?" His gaze narrowed. "He's doing very well. That's why you came to see me? Because of your brother?"

The warmth he'd greeted her with had vanished. The smiling eyes had been replaced with blue chips of ice.

She backtracked hastily. "No, no, I just asked." Now he must think her a total mother hen. Forcing a conciliatory smile, she said, "I'm pleased he's getting on well."

Callum rose to his feet. "I've been intending to suggest that he apply for one of the scholarships that Ironstone offers." His cold gaze swept her. "And before you leap to any nasty conclusions, this is an opportunity offered to any school-leavers who work for us to go to university. I don't even administer it."

She'd done it now. She'd made him mad. And if she breathed a word about the car Adrian had crashed, her brother would not only lose his vacation job and the chance of a permanent position, he'd also lose all chance of a scholarship—and it would be her fault.

To placate him, she said, "It would be the answer to my prayers." And it was true. The thought of Adrian studying toward a career. Having a chance of a successful future...

Except it would come from the Ironstone family. But she could live with that. She certainly wouldn't stand in Adrian's way.

Yet before she could say anything further, Callum continued, "So if you didn't come to accept my invitation and you didn't come see me about your brother, why are you here?"

Help. She sucked in a deep breath. There was only one thing left to say—sure, it meant she'd have to eat crow, but she could do that.

"I wanted to thank you for giving me the

chance to cater for you." Her stomach heaved. "I've already had a call as a result. Look." She dug into her bag and pulled out a few of the business cards she'd had printed up yesterday. "One of your dinner guests on Saturday asked for a card. I didn't have any. So I've had some printed up. What do you think?" She couldn't restrain the lilt of pride in her voice as she passed him a card.

He studied it. "Not bad. Do you have any more?"

"Why?"

"I might be able to hand them to prospective clients." He shot her a quick glance. "In fact, can you cater a Christmas cocktail party?" Callum rattled off a sum per head. "In the boardroom here? This Friday?"

Embarrassment squirmed through her. "That wasn't a hint. I didn't mean for you to give me more—"

"The caterer we booked has fallen ill. Do you want the job? Or do I get Biddy to find someone else?"

Miranda considered Adrian's predicament. Their tight finances. "Perhaps," she said cautiously.

A rap on the door had Callum stepping away from her. "Yes or no?" He parodied her question from earlier, and Miranda flushed.

Biddy popped her head around the doorjamb. "The copies are done, and everyone's finished their coffee—they're waiting for you."

He moved toward the door. "So what will it be?"

Ignoring the receptionist's curious glance, Miranda blew out the breath she'd been holding. "Yes."

Five

The boardroom was packed.

Everywhere Callum looked people held cocktail glasses, while they talked and laughed. Waitresses in long, red sequined dresses wearing Santa hats with fur trim offered around trays of snacks. And behind the hum of conversation he could hear the festive notes of "Ding Dong Merrily on High."

He should've been pleased. Ecstatic, in fact. Yet all he could do was glare in increasing frustration at the woman who'd pulled it all off.

Miranda had chosen to wear fishnets.

Callum really hadn't needed his brother, Fraser, to point that out to him. She wore black. A snug dress that, unlike the V-neck of last week's dress, had a high collar suited to a nun and should've looked seriously sedate. He couldn't take his eyes off her as she busied herself around the buffet table piled with mince pies and pots of whipped cream, repositioning the posies of poinsettias tied with gold bows and lit up with red candles.

Did the fishnets, too, end at the tops of her thighs?

A bolt of raw lust stabbed him at the memory of stroking the soft skin of her inner thigh. Had she worn them deliberately to drive him out of his mind?

As for that damn frilly white apron that tied with the great white bow behind her back, begging him to yank it loose...

Ah, hell.

"Back off," Callum growled as he caught Fraser smiling at Miranda for the second time in less than five minutes.

"I'm pulling rank," Fraser murmured. "I'm older. Go away."

Callum forced his attention from the woman who had him tied up in mental knots. "Forget it," he told his brother grimly. "That doesn't work anymore."

"You're warning me off!" Fraser's grin widened as he searched Callum's face. "I thought you were already attached." Turning his head, Fraser scanned the room. "Although I haven't seen the princess here tonight."

"Petra doesn't like it when you call her Princess," he said pompously, and spoiled the effect by slicing his brother a dirty look.

"Does your lack of answer mean she was supposed to be here?"

"No."

Callum shuddered at the memory of the disastrous call he'd made from New York. He should have ended it with Petra a week ago. It hadn't been fair to keep Petra on a string, not while this hunger for Miranda ate at him like acid. Petra hadn't said much, but he knew he'd hurt her. *It's not you, it's me*—he'd even used that old corny line. *You deserve better.* She did—he should've waited to break it off with her in person.

So he'd organized a string of pearls to be delivered to her, more to assuage his guilt than to offer consolation. And he was grateful Petra wasn't here tonight—although he'd noted Gordon's appearance with some relief.

Callum knew he probably had Petra to thank for that. The woman had style.

So why the hell couldn't it be Petra he craved with this deep and desperate desire?

"She's got more sense than I credited her with if she dumped you." Fraser sounded almost satisfied.

Narrowing his gaze, Callum studied his brother's mocking smile. He didn't correct his brother's mistaken belief that it was Petra who'd done the ditching. Instead he said with brotherly candor, "I don't think she likes you much. Kind of like Miranda—who hates my guts."

"Miranda?" Fraser's suddenly blank expression gave nothing away. "Wasn't Thomas Owen's daughter named Miranda?"

Without meaning to, Callum glanced toward the woman who'd been tormenting his nights. "Yes."

Fraser followed his gaze. "That same Miranda?"

This time Callum's "Yes" was terse.

Knowing his brother was examining him with keen interest made Callum feel uncomfortably exposed. The silence stretched long enough to become pointed. Finally Fraser said gently, "Ouch."

Exactly. "Just stay away from her."

"And if I don't?" Fraser asked. "Then what, little brother? You'll beat me to pulp?"

Blood rushed through his ears. "Don't... try...it." He bit the words out with aggressive intent.

Fraser hooted in disbelief. "You *would*."

The sound of his sibling's laughter caused Callum to ask grimly, "What's so damn funny?"

"If you don't know, I'm not telling." Fraser was already off to where their half brothers,

Jack and Hunter, huddled with a major stake-holder. Still smirking, he threw over his shoulder, "You always did like to do things the hard way, Callum."

You always did like to do things the hard way. Fraser's words still rang in Callum's ears as he fought his way through the crush of people that seemed to have grown larger and louder over the past hour, heading to where Miranda and two waitresses were replenishing platters of savories on the temporary bar.

She shot him a wary look as he approached.

He supposed it was foolish to have hoped for a little gratitude after all the trouble he'd taken to ensure she could do the catering tonight. Biddy had been far from pleased at having to call the catering company that had already been booked—he'd had to pay them in full for the late cancellation.

Of course Miranda didn't know that. He'd told her the caterer had been forced to renege for reasons of illness.... Nor did she know he'd broken up with Petra. He had no intention of telling her either. Miranda already had more power over him than he liked.

Talk about a tangled web.

As far as doing things the hard way, this fierce attraction to Miranda topped all. Callum wasn't even sure his motives were pure any longer. What had begun as a sop to his conscience had somehow gotten out of control since meeting the all-grown-up Miranda. He didn't know what had hit him. All he knew was that he wanted to take her back to his bed…sate himself with her.

Hell, why should she be grateful? Given her conviction that he'd caused her father's death it wasn't surprising she couldn't bear the sight of him. Callum didn't like the niggle of discomfort that ate at his stomach—the same sensation that often gnawed in the middle of the night. If he hadn't pushed so hard to have Thomas Owen arrested, the man might still be alive today.

And Miranda and Adrian would still have a father.

As he cut through the throng, he smiled and

nodded to business acquaintances but didn't pause until he reached Miranda, busy setting out serviettes and fresh bowls of olives amid a crowd at the bar.

"Need any help?"

Miranda's eyelashes fluttered down, blocking her eyes from his view. White serviettes printed with gold snowflakes fanned out under the touch of her deft fingers, and he had to strain his ears to hear her response.

"It's all under control."

He dropped his gaze from those teasing fingers. Only to be confronted by the provocative white apron with its starchy ruffles and wished furiously he could as easily control his wild thoughts. Clearing his throat, he managed, "Uh…I need to update you on Adrian."

Her hands stilled. "Adrian?"

The rest of what she said was drowned out by a burst of laughter. Not even staring at her mouth helped him make out the words— although the soft shape of her lips caused another quake of lust.

Placing a hand under her elbow, he drew her away from the bar. "Sorry, I can't hear you."

She came slowly, her arm suddenly stiff under his fingertips.

It didn't augur well for the chances of assuaging the growing hunger that burned in him. He bent forward and said loudly over the music and surrounding chatter, "Let me introduce you around—we can talk about Adrian later."

He sensed her hesitation. Flicking him a quick, sideways look, she rested a hand on his shoulder and rose on tiptoe. "I'm not sure I can wait."

Callum shuddered as her breath warmed his ear with the innocently provocative words. Turning his head, he discovered her mouth not far from his. For a moment he was tempted to throw caution to the winds. To confess that Petra meant nothing to him and that she, Miranda, consumed his every thought. To plunder the soft ripeness of that sweet mouth.

But she withdrew her hand, leaving him bereft. Bringing himself back to the present, he mouthed, "Later. We'll talk when the party settles down. Right now, I ought to circulate."

She glanced around at the press of people that made it impossible to talk and nodded, but her irises had darkened with worry.

"Adrian's fine," he said. Miranda needed to think more about herself and spend less time fretting about her brother. Into a short lull he said, "Have you got your business cards here?"

She nodded. "In my bag. I'll get them."

He gave her a thumbs-up and waited for her to return.

Once it had sunk in that Adrian's secret was still safe, Miranda's heartbeat steadied and she started to relax.

Callum introduced her to an older couple, Madge and Tom Murray. On learning that Miranda was responsible for the food, Madge said, "The mince pies simply melted in my mouth. What magic did you use?"

That launched a discussion about pastry that attracted a nearby woman. After several minutes

Miranda turned to Callum and Madge's husband and apologized profusely. "Sorry, I lose time when the talk is about food."

"Madge likes nothing more." Tom laughed.

The conversation moved on to favorite dishes and dinner-party disasters. Madge was amusing, and her husband clearly doted on her—even though he confessed to hating oysters which Madge vowed was grounds for divorce.

As everyone laughed, Miranda felt a stab of envy. Even though her father had adored and indulged Flo, there'd never been this sense of kinship and shared laughter between her parents.

The arrival of a tall, dark-haired man who looked vaguely familiar interrupted her thoughts. But the respite proved to be short. The newcomer turned out to be none other than Callum's brother, Fraser, whose sharp eyes assessed Miranda and missed nothing. Not the fact that his brother stood beside her, nor that his brother's arm was behind her. His arched brows rose a little, but thankfully he only added to the hilarity in their discussions about food.

"What is your secret food passion, Miranda?" asked Madge.

"Chocolate," she said. "Rich, dark and slightly bitter."

"Sounds like Callum," Fraser said with a sly grin.

Miranda didn't dare glance at the silent man standing next to her. In an instant those mad moments in his home played through her brain like a movie in slow motion.

Callum hoisting her up and stepping between her thighs. Callum soaping her in the shower afterward. Callum naked and damp with droplets moving over her before pinning her on his bed and...

She became brutally aware of the gentle pressure of his hand resting in the small of her back. And blinked. Hard.

This was Callum Ironstone, for heaven's sake. Petra's almost financé. Her brother's boss. Her sworn enemy. How could she allow such treacherous desires to consume her? How could she even be tempted to respond to his touch?

And worse, to every breath he drew? Yet the touch of his hand on her back seemed so…right. What was *wrong* with her?

"I need to get back to the kitchen," she said desperately, shifting out from beneath his hand.

"Don't you dare say anything about a woman's place," Madge warned as Fraser looked as if he were about to comment.

He said, "I wouldn't dare. Mother would send us to our rooms for voicing such heresy, wouldn't she, Callum?"

"Without a doubt." The laugh lines around Callum's eyes crinkled, making him even more attractive.

Miranda escaped before she could be further seduced. Or, heaven help her, admit that she *wanted* to be seduced.

Drat the man.

The long night was almost over.

Miranda had been clock-watching for the past half hour, waiting for the guests to leave as the medley of cheerful Christmas carols segued into light classics. But she still started when Callum came up silently behind her, invading the refuge she'd sought behind the tall Christmas tree in the lobby where she'd hidden in the hope of avoiding him.

A quick upward glance from where she knelt beside three crates revealed that he'd discarded his jacket, and the white shirt he wore was startling in the dim lobby.

"I've been looking for you." Callum held out a glass of what looked like port. "You've done enough tonight, Miranda. Leave packing those glasses and take a break."

She glanced at the dark liquid swirling in the crystal glass and pictured—too vividly—what had happened the last time she'd indulged in wine under his roof. Her pulse quickened, causing blood to rush to her head and a wave of dizzy desire.

"No, thanks." Miranda fought to control her physical reaction. Port would only cause her defenses—already vulnerable—to crumble more rapidly. Earlier he'd promised to catch her later and talk about Adrian; no doubt that was why he had been looking for her. Not to seduce her—contrary to her wild imaginings.

He shrugged and took a sip of his wine. The lights of the tall Christmas tree overhead flashed, creating a surreal glow of silver, and for a moment she was riveted. His tie had been abandoned and the pulse in the hollow of his throat beat visibly.

She stared transfixed.

Then he surprised her.

"Tonight was a success. I want to thank you, Miranda."

His eyes were warm, the blue muted, making her wish they'd met under different circumstances—that he wasn't the man responsible for her father's death.

"I only did what you employed me to do," she said stiffly as he set his glass down on the white marble floor beside her. She ducked her head, determined not to reveal her impossible thoughts, and carried on stacking empty glasses into their crates, using the occasional ting of crystal as a warning bell to keep herself from falling under his thrall.

"No, you did far more than expected. The Christmas crackers were a success, and so were the edible Christmas tree decorations."

His voice came closer and she spoke quickly, desperate to keep him at bay. "I thought your guests might like something to take home."

"Madge Murray was raving about the chocolate angels."

"Yes, I gave her extras." She raised her shoulders and let them fall with what she hoped looked like a careless shrug. "My mother taught me how to make them when I was a little girl." Flo had always had the ability to bake fairy-tale items; it was the ordinary things like lunch and dinner that were beyond her.

At the brush of Callum's fingers under her chin, her head came up in a hurry. He pinned her under his ferociously bright gaze. As the Christmas lights flickered overhead, she imagined the glitter in his eyes revealed emotion. But the words he spoke negated that fancy.

"Her husband is one of our most important customers."

The hope she'd glimpsed died. Of course, for Callum everything was always about work. Never about emotion. Or fairy tales. He was ready to marry for corporate convenience. Unlike her, he would never believe in love…or Christmas wishes. She tried not to let her disappointment show—and hated herself for wishing it had all been about so much more, and that the emotion she'd imagined she'd glimpsed had been real.

She drew away. "I'm glad you're pleased."

"Very pleased."

"Good." She got to her feet. "Now I'd better get these glasses to the collection point. The company I hired them from will be here soon to fetch them."

Callum stared at the woman with frustration. He wasn't interested in the damn dirty glasses. Why couldn't she be one of those kittenish women who batted her eyelids and cooed her thanks? How he would revel being on the receiving end of her gratitude….

He took in the creamy skin, the soft, lush mouth and desire spiked through him.

Dark. Driving. Relentless.

Callum gave himself a mental shake. Not going to happen. Not tonight. Not ever. So he'd better get over this…this fascination she held for him.

Even Fraser had noticed.

Hell.

Would he ever be able to get that night she'd spent in his bed out his head? Or stop thinking about how to get her back there and make love to her all over again?

He must be crazy.

Especially as she was making it clear as the crystal she was packing away that she had no intention of even dating him. All night she'd been running from him, apprehension in her eyes. And how could he blame her? He'd been reduced to using his company functions as a way to spend time with her.

Once the festive season was over it would be

some time before he could set up catering engagements for her without arousing her suspicion. He would have no excuse to see her, not unless he took to frequenting The Golden Goose.

He grimaced. That would be desperate measures indeed.

"What's wrong?"

He straightened at the sound of Miranda's voice. "Wrong?"

"You're frowning."

"I've no reason to frown—it's been a very successful evening."

"Good."

He told himself he'd find another way to keep in touch with her. "Oh, earlier I wanted to tell you that I spoke to your brother."

A subtle tension shimmered through her. If he hadn't been so aware of every nuance and change in her expressive eyes, he probably wouldn't even have noticed.

"After I flew in from New York I gave him the application forms for the two Ironstone Insurance scholarships and told him that I'd nominate him." His nomination would carry a lot of weight with the deciding committee, but she didn't need to know that. It would only make her believe he was merely giving charity in another guise.

Yet for once, instead of objecting, the tension seemed to drain out of her. "If Adrian could get a scholarship to university—or even a job for next year—it would be such a relief." Her lashes fluttered down. "Thank you."

It must strangle her to have to thank him for anything. He reached out and touched her arm, intending to tell her that she owed him no thanks—that it was the least he could do.

And froze.

Here was the opportunity he'd been looking for. So perfect—and he'd almost missed it. He could use her brother as a way to keep in touch— arrange meetings with her to talk about him.

All to get into Miranda's pants again, he scoffed at himself.

Was this what he had been reduced to? Miranda's brother was almost a man and Callum had always tried to treat him like an adult. If

Adrian found out Callum was meeting Miranda to discuss him, the bond he'd been working so hard to forge with the youth would be broken.

But right now he couldn't care about that.

Unless he offered Adrian a permanent position at Ironstone Insurance or called in a favor to make sure her brother was offered a university scholarship, there would be no more reason to see Miranda.

No excuse to lure her into his bed….

He let the thumb resting on her arm stroke along the fabric of her dress sleeve and heard her breath catch.

Not totally unaffected then.

He couldn't help remembering how soft her naked skin had been against his, how sweet she'd tasted. His gaze rested on her mouth.

So passionate.

This craving for her confounded him. He'd been right to break it off with Petra—he couldn't marry any woman while he felt like this. And despite Miranda's determined indifference, he suspected she wanted him every bit as badly. The passion she'd revealed the night they'd made love couldn't be feigned.

If only her father's death didn't stand between them.

"Miranda, about your father…"

The lights flashed and he read anger in her eyes. "You should never have—"

"I had no choice."

"There's always a choice," she said.

She was right. He'd been determined to prove how tough he was, how merciless. The corporate tycoon. It was something he'd have to live with all his life.

"You're right."

"Thank you."

For a long moment he thought she was going to say more.

But instead she said with forced cheerfulness, "Christmas will soon be here. I'll just have to wish that everything will come right for Adrian in the coming year."

He blinked. "You think Christmas wishes work?"

She tipped her head up and stared at the tree above them. "I think one can dream…and wish…and hope."

Miranda was a romantic. For a moment he wished for her sheer, blind optimism. Unable to help himself, he asked, "What do you look forward to most at Christmas?"

"I love spending it with my family. I love—" She broke off. "You don't want to hear all this."

"But I do." And he found he was telling the truth. "Tell me what you want to see when you wake up on Christmas morning."

"The best gift?" She gave him a funny little twisted smile. "Well, I can't have that. So I'll take snow. As much as I love the lights in the city at Christmas, I love snow more. And it doesn't often snow in London for Christmas. Sleet and sludge, yes, but not pure, pristine snow that crunches underfoot in the early morning and yours are the first footprints of the day."

He heard the longing. "You miss the country, don't you?"

"Particularly at this time of the year."

The lights in the Christmas tree flashed again, revealing a wistful, faraway expression he knew she'd have hated him to see.

"I remember as a child getting up on Christmas morning, going with Adrian to check our stockings on the mantelpiece. Then I'd go and see my pony—take the biggest carrots I could find and slices of apple." She gave a whisper of a sigh. "The warm smell of horse and hay inside the stables after the crisp air outside…that must be one of my favorite Christmas memories. And by the time I got back to the house my parents would be awake and we'd all gather under the tree."

Her lashes lay in dark crescents against her cheeks, and her mouth curved up in a smile that made an unfamiliar ache tighten around his chest.

"A real tree." She gestured to the Christmas tree that towered over them. "Not a fake monstrosity with fake snow like this one."

Callum nodded, feeling a strange affinity for her. When he was growing up, his family had always decorated a pine tree, too. And each year the scent had filled his home along with the sweet aromas of baking biscuits. They still shared Christmas in the country every year.

He wanted to offer her a chance to relive the Christmas she dreamed of. He wanted to invite her home to spend Christmas in the country with him at Fairwinds. Although he suspected she would refuse his invitation.

"Miranda—"

She reached up to straighten a silver bow on the company tree. The movement pulled her dress tight across her breasts and his breath caught in his throat. He forgot what he'd been about to say. Forgot everything except the crazy hunger she made him feel.

Unable to resist, he hooked an arm around her and pulled her close. Then he brushed his lips across hers very gently.

The air grew still.

Callum wanted to kiss her again with all the pent-up passion she'd kindled in him and sweep her off her feet before carrying her to his home.

Instead he set her away from him.

She touched her mouth with two fingers. "What was that for?"

There had to be a reason for him to kiss her? Callum gave her a long look. Instead of collapsing into his arms like most women would have, the suspicion in her eyes deepened.

Finally he said, "Blame it on the mistletoe."

She glanced upward and a puzzled frown creased her brow. "But there isn't any."

Exactly. He needed no excuse to kiss her—the fire she'd ignited burned with an unquenchable fury—but Callum doubted she'd appreciate his honesty if he told her that.

Six

Miranda didn't appreciate the way Callum was messing with her head. That feather-of-a-kiss-that-had-hardly-been-a-kiss had shaken her.

Badly.

And even a busy weekend at The Golden Goose failed to give her respite to regain her composure. All because the man in question turned up at the Goose on Saturday and ordered lunch.

Miranda had known about Callum's arrival in minutes. Kitty, the youngest, prettiest and flightiest of the waitresses, had rushed into the kitchen to share that the most gorgeous guy she'd seen in her life had just walked in.

"Tall, dark and with periwinkle-blue eyes," she gushed. "He looks like a movie star."

"In the Goose?" But despite her skepticism Miranda's heart stopped in horror. She steadied herself. That description could apply to thousands of men. Well, maybe not thousands. But it didn't mean…

Yet she hadn't been able to resist taking a peek—just to make sure.

Only to discover it *was* Callum.

He sat alone at a small round table to the side of the gas fireplace. In the middle of the day the fire flickered, but the flames still gave off much-needed warmth. Callum's dark head was bent over the menu, but he looked up almost as though he'd sensed her stare.

She drew quickly out of sight, hissing at her stupidity under her breath.

While Mick muttered about chefs who had too little work, Miranda hurried to rescue a batch of brandy snaps from the oven before they burnt to crisp and, after rolling them deftly around the handle of a wooden spoon, set about piping whipped cream flavored with Grand Marnier into the now-crisp tubes.

What did Callum want? Why was he here?

Her hands shook as she squeezed the piping bag and cream oozed everywhere. Which made her want to kill him!

"He wants steak." Kitty bounced into the kitchen. "Rare. No sauce. And battered onion rings. A real, live carnivore."

The two other girls giggled. "I'll take him some water," one said.

"Maybe he wants extra onions." And the second followed her out for a closer inspection.

Miranda stopped herself from rolling her eyes. For the next thirty minutes she was aware of the giggles as the waitresses vied to serve him, and it irritated her beyond belief.

The final insult came when Kitty delivered his request to convey his thanks in person to the dessert chef.

All too conscious of Gianni glowering,

Miranda allowed herself to be dragged out into the limelight, noting Callum's lack of surprise when she appeared.

Of course he'd known she was here.

Resisting the urge to drop a facetious curtsy, she smiled sweetly. "I'm so pleased you enjoyed your meal."

His gaze rested on her lips, causing them to tingle, before lifting to study her. "What are you doing for Christmas this year?"

Miranda gave a small sigh. "What I always do—spend it with my family."

For a moment she thought he was going to ask her something, but he only said, "My mother has a passion for brandy snaps, and these are quite the best I've ever eaten."

His sincerity took her aback. He was looking at her like he wanted to devour her. Miranda couldn't have spoken if she'd tried.

"She would love these."

"I'll let you have the recipe," she croaked at last.

Tipping his head to one side, he considered her. "I'd rather you made them for her."

Miranda thought about it, her heart quickening. What did he mean? That he wanted her to meet his mother? Then common sense kicked in. Unlikely. "But she doesn't live in London. The biscuit would go soggy. They should be eaten fresh."

He was shaking his head. "It was a dumb idea."

"What was?" she asked, puzzled, wondering what she'd missed.

"Coming here!" He gave her a lopsided smile. "But next time Mother is in town, I will hold you to that offer."

His smile widened, holding no edge or hint of seduction, and for the first time Miranda got a glimpse of the man his family saw.

And it was a different person from the man she'd grown to loathe. This man she could like. Yet she was no closer to knowing why he'd come today. And she'd turned down his offer to go to *Les Misérables* with him tonight—and maybe get to know him better. There was no point wondering if Petra was enjoying herself. Thay way lay the path to heartache. She'd sensibly refuse his invitation. The man was an enigma—she would never understand him.

The rest of the weekend was an anticlimax with Gianni stamping and snorting like a bull and glaring balefully across the kitchen at Miranda. One of the girls must have told him what Callum had said, and he hadn't liked it.

Thankfully, when Miranda finally got home late in the rainy cold of Sunday night there were no flowers to welcome her and remind her of her disturbing nemesis that she couldn't seem to keep out of her life.

With Adrian still out, the little terrace house seemed empty. Entering the dining room, Miranda saw Flo hurriedly sliding a window envelope under a file.

"Another bill?" she asked, picking up her pace as she crossed to where her mother sat at the table. "I thought I'd paid everything."

"No, no, don't you worry about this, darling." The vagueness in her mother's tone sharpened Miranda's interest. "Let me see—I might have paid it already."

"This is mine."

"Yours?" She looked at her mother in surprise.

Flo normally gave all her bills to Miranda to pay—she was hopeless at organizing her finances. Though it tended to require the conjuring up of money from nowhere—often hard-worked overtime—to meet them.

Miranda felt sick. "Please, not more overdue bills that I don't know about."

Snagging up the corner of the file, Miranda caught sight of the name of an exclusive department store on the bill under the envelope. "Hemingway's?"

Guilt glinted in Flo's dark eyes. "I needed a new coat."

Miranda pulled out the piece of paper and then blanched. "What was it? Mink?"

"Don't be silly, darling." Her mother whipped the bill out from between her nerveless fingers. "There were also a few fripperies for my winter wardrobe. Your father wouldn't have wanted to see me dressed in rags."

"Dad isn't here anymore—and we don't have his income." She spied another bill from the same store, dated the previous month. "*Pans?* You told me your friend Sorrell gave those to you."

Her mother flushed, an ugly stain on her pale skin. "I'll deal with the bills, Miranda."

"How?"

Putting her hands on her hips, Miranda considered her mother. Apart from the allowance Callum paid her mother—the amount Miranda had been led to believe came from the carefully invested residue of her father's estate—Flo had no income.

"I'll make arrangements, darling. Don't worry about it. I'm not useless."

Arrangements? Dread curled in Miranda's stomach. "What kind of arrangements?"

"I'll call up Hemingway's and have them grant me an indulgence—they've done it before."

"Done it before?" asked Miranda, trying to make sense of why the store would grant her mother an extension on her accounts.

"Yes—last time they even gave me a bigger credit limit."

Miranda stared at her vague, sweet mother with mounting horror. "Increased your credit limit when you aren't paying your bills? Why would they do that?"

Flo looked abashed. "Because of Callum, of course."

"Because of Callum?" She must sound like the village idiot the way she kept repeating her mother. "What does Callum Ironstone have to do with your accounts?"

"He originally settled all our accounts after your father died. It was part of our agreement," Flo said defensively. "Everyone knows who the Ironstones are. Things were so difficult at the time—don't you remember? He used to pay the accounts I sent him until you took over."

Her mother fluttered her hands like a delicate butterfly but Miranda refused to be diverted. "I don't remember. It must have been in that agreement you never showed me," she said grimly.

"Are you telling me you've extended your credit on the basis of Callum's name?" It was too horrible to contemplate.

"Well, it's not costing him anything," Flo said defiantly.

"But it will if you don't pay. I can't believe these stores have let the balances run on for so long."

"I call them regularly—I'm hardly some debtor they think is about to abscond. They know Callum will look after me."

This was getting worse and worse. Miranda snatched the account back, and studied it, before looking back at her mother in despair. "The interest is running at a prohibitive rate."

"I don't think *all* the stores charge such high rates, darling."

All the stores? "There are more?" Miranda stared at her mother, aghast.

So much for her stubborn determination *never* to be beholden to Callum again. There was no money to pay these accounts. Callum would be contacted by the stores eventually to be told that her mother was shopping on his credit.

Unless of course Hemingway's decided to institute legal action to recover the debt.

The shame of it.

"Oh, dear Lord, Mum. What have you done?"

It was the following afternoon—her day off—and after a spending the day walking aimlessly around the city, her brain in turmoil, Miranda finally decided to take action about her mother's revelation.

Even if Callum had paid off her parents' accounts after her father's death, he could hardly have intended her mother to continue using his name to lever credit. The time had come to see him and lay all the dead cats on his boardroom table, she decided with mordant humor. Adrian and Flo would have to put up with whatever repercussions followed.

She could no longer continue deceiving him.

Miranda paused at Trafalgar Square. Years ago Flo had sometimes brought her and Adrian here to feed the pigeons, and each Christmas, they'd come to admire the lights and Christmas tree. The pigeons had long since been discouraged, but the Christmas tree still stood. And the fountain Adrian had almost fallen into one icy winter's day.

So when her cell phone rang and she heard Callum's distinctive voice, Miranda was hardly surprised. She sank down on a bench near the fountain. To her annoyance her "Hi" was more than a little breathless.

"Been making any brandy snaps lately?"

His lighthearted comment made her want to cry. That teasing humor wouldn't last once he heard what her mother had been up to. "Not enough."

That reminded her that she needed to organize some overtime. There were Flo's accounts to pay. On the spur of the moment she said rashly, "I don't suppose you have more work for me?"

The pause echoed in her ears.

She shut her eyes. Stupid. She opened them and gazed blindly at the tall tree decorated with vertical rows of light on the other side of the fountain. "I mean real work. I don't want a donation."

"I know you don't. I was thinking."

She tried not to notice how low his voice was…how sexy…or how it sent shivers down her spine.

"Maybe we could meet and talk about people I know who might be able to give you work," he said.

It wouldn't be a date. And little as she wanted to be in his debt, what harm was there in using his social network to further her own ends? It wasn't as if she was taking money from him.

And she would use the opportunity to tell him what Flo had done. Maybe even what Adrian had done—if the meeting went smoothly enough.

"That would be great." The world seemed bright and shiny—no longer dull and gray. "I'd like that."

"Then I'll pick you up on Friday—we'll have dinner."

Friday night? That sounded suspiciously like a date. But she knew that this time she wouldn't refuse.

Callum was rather pleased with himself.

Not only had he managed to secure a date

with Miranda—although he rather doubted she'd view the evening in the same light—he'd also gotten glowing feedback about the Christmas cocktail party Miranda had catered for him. Apart from the fact that everyone had enjoyed it, saying it was streets ahead of any similar event they'd attended, Hunter told him there'd been a promise of a new corporate deal from Tom Murray, and a businessman Callum had been courting for a long time had made an appointment to talk about having all his plants insured with Ironstone Insurance. He'd even heard that Miranda had catered a small dinner party for Hunter, though she'd said nothing about that.

All in all Callum had the feeling that his plans were finally working out.

When he picked her up on Friday evening, she was ready for him, auguring well for the night. He liked punctuality in a woman.

No black dress this time—he didn't know whether to be sorry or relieved. Instead she wore a pair of fitted narrow-legged black pants, high boots and a skirted coat with a wide belt that covered her curves. No matter. He had every intention of taking her somewhere warm, so by the end of the evening she would be wearing far fewer clothes if it all went to plan.

Seated opposite her at a table in the alcove of the bay window in one of his favorite restaurants, Callum smiled in satisfaction as he took in the sensual sheen of the gray satin blouse she wore. So far so good. He watched as she studied the menu, that endearing frown furrowing her brow. When she snapped the menu shut, she caught him staring. Callum raised his champagne flute and took a quick sip.

"Why are you looking at me like that?"

"You do things with so much concentration—it takes your whole being." He set the glass down on the white linen cloth.

Miranda looked down and fiddled with her fork. She looked embarrassed as she said, "Some people say I'm too single-minded."

"Nothing wrong with that."

"You think?" She abandoned the fork, and

her gaze locked with his. "I've been told it's unfeminine."

He chuckled. "There's not an unfeminine bone in your body." His gaze traced the dark brows, the gentle curve of her cheek and settled on her lush mouth. Her tongue came out and moistened her bottom lip. Callum quickly raised his eyes. She was staring at him, her dark eyes wide and a little shocked.

There was no doubt that he must've revealed some of the insatiable hunger she roused in him.

To play down the moment, he couldn't resist asking, "Why are you looking at me like that?"

"No reason." She flushed and glanced away, picking up her serviette and spreading it out before laying it on her lap. The heat that smoldered whenever he was near her ignited.

Miranda was every bit as aware of him as he was of her. He wished she would give in to the inevitable. Couldn't she see they were destined to be lovers?

Then she looked up. "For some reason this

feels like a date." She pointed at the tall crystal flutes and the arrangement of white roses on the table. "I told you I didn't want to date you." But a slight smile softened her words.

A waiter arrived and lit the squat white candle with a taper, before taking their orders.

Once he'd topped their glasses and collected the menus he departed, Callum took up the conversation where they'd left off. "It's not a date—it's a business meeting."

He fought back a grin at her expression of disbelief.

She snorted. "You bring business colleagues here on a Friday night?"

He raised his hands in a gesture of innocence. "I've been known to invite business associates on a Saturday night for dinner—I'm a busy man."

"I accept you'd bring your brothers here. But what about Gordon? Or Tom Murray? Tom must love the champagne, huh?" She raised her glass in a mock salute.

This time he couldn't help the grin that spread

over his face. "We do celebrate business ventures sometimes."

Miranda set her glass down. "And mergers?"

Quietly he said, "I told Petra our relationship was over."

The mood changed. All lighthearted banter stilled. A sizzling tension filled the space between them.

"You broke up with her?" Dismay darkened the caramel eyes to a shade of chocolate. "I never wanted that."

"Over a week ago."

An unreadable expression flashed across her face. *"Over a week ago?"* she asked. "And you said nothing?"

"It had nothing to do with you," he lied.

It had everything to do with Miranda. He'd been very content with the notion of settling down with Petra until Miranda came along and stirred up his libido, leaving him hungering for so much more. They were so good together. Yet she stubbornly refused to acknowledge that…he could pretend, too, if that's what he wanted.

Callum leaned forward. "This is a meeting. And don't let the champagne bother you—it's tax deductible."

"Tax deductible?" Miranda scoffed, but the annoyance had ebbed and, to his relief, amusement lurked behind the shadows in her eyes.

He was winning. Time to cut the ground from under her feet while he was still ahead. "Let's get to work, and see how I can help you with your business. I hear you catered very successfully for Hunter last week."

Her features grew animated. "Oh, yes, I've been meaning to thank you for the referral."

"It was nothing." With a wave of his hand, he dismissed it. "Hunter was impressed."

"One of his guests called earlier today and asked me for a quote for a New Year's Eve party."

"Word of mouth. The best way to get known."

"It's an enormous relief. If I can make this work…" She fell silent.

He waited.

Finally she gave a soft sigh. "Things have been… tense at The Golden Goose. I'm not sure how much longer I'll have a job. With the economic climate there has been talk of re-trenchments."

It surprised him that she'd chosen to confide in him. Normally she worked so hard to keep him at arm's length. "You won't be affected."

She nibbled her lip. "I wish I could be so certain."

Callum got the sense she didn't share personal fears easily. "What makes you think that? You're overqualified for that place, you're diligent." He leaned back. "And you cook like a dream."

She gave him a quick smile. "Thanks for the vote of confidence. I've stayed at the Goose because of the convenience—it's close to home. But I'm the junior chef—and the other chef makes life hard."

"I get it. You're young. You're good at what you do. And you probably don't earn what he does. I'm not surprised you threaten him."

Spreading her hands, she said, "Maybe you're right. I've wondered if it's that. But it doesn't help that whenever there are accidents in the

kitchen, Gianni always manages to blame me—
even if I was somewhere else. Not to mention
the times he tells Mick I'm late when I arrive
bang on time."

"You don't need to put up with it. You could get
a much better job if you wanted. In a place like
this." He gestured to the fine white linen and sparkling silverware on their table, then waved his
arm to encompass the rest of the restaurant with
its elegant high ceilings, bay windows and
alcoves, and the ivory curtains draped in swags.

"Can I? There's a cloud over my father.
People remember scandals like embezzlement.
They worry about the fruit not falling far from
the tree." There was no bitterness in her voice.

"You'd have references."

"Really?" She raised an eyebrow. "What kind
of a reference would I get?" Her expression
was skeptical. "Gianni and the boss are
friends—they even flat together."

Callum resisted the impulse to tell her that *he*
would supply a reference to any restaurant she
chose. He suspected she'd rather do things her

own way. "Then focus on the catering business that Adrian says you've always dreamed of. You've already made a start. Have you got a business plan?"

She nodded.

"I'll look at it if you want." He drew an envelope from his pocket. "Here's a list of names with contact numbers of executives I know who would be more than happy to give you work. Go the whole way."

Hesitantly she took the list from him, unfolding it to glance through the names. From her expression he knew that she'd recognized several of them as movers and shakers in the city.

"I've already contacted most of them to let them know you'll be calling them."

"It's not that easy," she protested. "I'd planned to ease in gradually, but times are hard. Even established businesses are failing, and I have responsibilities."

Despite her confident façade, Miranda was afraid. Something inside him cracked a little. "The last name is an accountant who'll be able to steer you through the pitfalls of running a small business—she's an old friend of our family."

There was an expression in her eyes he couldn't read. Was she thinking of her family? Her father? Was she blaming him for how her father's death had landed her in this position?

Again that smothering sense of guilt closed in on him. She shouldn't have borne it all alone.

He'd tried to help—to ease the family's precarious financial position and give Miranda and her brother some sort of education. And now he was determined to help her get her catering business off the ground. But nothing could bring her father back.

He reached out and closed his hand over hers. "Let me help you."

She jerked away, clearly recoiling from the idea… from him.

He gave her a moment, then said, "You blame me for killing your father, so why is it so hard to let me sponsor you?"

"And make it easy for you? Throw money at the problem and your conscience is clean?" Her eyes sparkled with what he hoped was anger and not tears. "I don't think so."

He couldn't bear tears.

"My conscience will never be clear," he confessed.

She blinked frantically, then her shoulders slumped. "I wish Dad were here. Lately I've been wishing for that a lot."

Her raw admission caused an ache to splinter deep in his chest. He again tightened his hand around hers. She started, but didn't withdraw this time.

"I'm sorry, Miranda—more than you'll ever know."

Her eyes were full of anguished shadows. "Thank you. I needed to hear that."

He glanced at the list. "Call those names. You're going to be a success. And don't think what I'm doing for you is unique. I often give someone a break. And that's what we do with our company scholarships, too. Adrian's got a real chance to get one of those. He's hardworking and smart. No reason why he shouldn't."

Her eyelids lowered, veiling her gaze. "I appreciate your nominating Adrian. Now that he's finished school, he's going to have to think hard about his future."

"He's a big boy now. He has to make his own choices."

Her lashes fluttered up and she gave him a rapid, indecipherable glance, then sighed. "You're probably right. But I've been so used to looking out for him. Which brings me to something else I have to discuss with you tonight."

"What's that?"

"Flo."

"Your mother?"

She nodded. "She's been running up accounts all over the city. And the stores are letting her do it because they think you're guaranteeing her expenditure. You need to write to them so it can stop."

His fingers played with hers. "I can afford it."

She shook her head. "No. I'll never be able to repay you."

"I don't expect you to."

"Then I'd lose my self-respect. Please, Callum, let them know. I don't want to be further in your debt. It's going to be hard enough paying you back as it is."

"You don't have to pay me back."

"Of course I do." Cent by backbreaking cent.

A frown darkened his expression. "That's not what I ever intended."

"I know."

"So why don't you forget about it?"

She'd thought she could. But how could they ever move into any kind of relationship—even an uneasy friendship—if she owed him money? She'd forever feel indebted to him, some kind of charity case. She needed to be able to face him as an equal. The news that he'd broken up with Petra had caused her heart to leap. For a brief moment she'd entertained a wild hope of more than friendship…then she'd doused it.

She freed her hand from his. "I can't."

Originally it had been her hatred of Callum that had had her refusing his help. She'd wanted him to feel responsible—guilty even. But then she'd discovered he'd already spent so much she hadn't known about—on her, on her family—because he really had felt guilty about her father. And clearly still did. It didn't sit well with her that for almost three years she'd cursed him, hated him, wished that lightning would strike him.

Besides, if she accepted his money, Callum might view her in the same way that he must see her mother—pretty, but fundamentally a parasite.

"There's an easy way around all this," he said.

Nothing was ever easy. She gave him a suspicious look. "What?"

"We make a good team."

Miranda snorted. "Where did you get that idea from?"

"The Christmas cocktail function was a huge success. People loved it. And it's given me the opening to secure opportunities I've been trying to tie up for a long time." He drew her hand back into his. "I need a hostess."

It was part of the reason marrying Petra

would've been so convenient. But he'd never desired Petra with this raw, physical ache.

"I was hardly a hostess. I just made the food," she said dismissively.

He tipped his head to one side and considered her for a long moment. What was it about this woman that drew him? Even when he wasn't with her, all he could think about was her. She was starting to consume him. "No, you did so much more than that. It was the little touches that made the evening memorable." Even his PR officer had commented on the unique feel of the party.

He massaged her fingers and they went stiff beneath his. "You're asking me to hostess your functions?"

"More than that."

Suspicion glistened in her eyes at his throaty statement. "You're asking me to be your mistress?"

"No!" Even he wasn't fool enough to think she would accept such a preposterous proposition. But, God, he was tempted to ask. To have her in his bed, fulfilling his every desire…

Perhaps there was another option.

"So what *do* you want?"

Miranda had never been one to back away. So it was to be expected that she'd get to the crux of the matter. What did he want?

He lifted her rigid fingers to his mouth and placed a soft kiss on each fingertip, watching her eyes grow wide with shock.

"I suppose," he said slowly, "I'm asking you to be my wife."

Seven

"Your *wife?"*

Miranda's lips parted in astonishment and her pulse picked up. Opposite her, Callum looked almost as startled by his proposal as she. Had he meant to ask? Or was this an impulsive mistake? Her brain worked furiously. Did his proposal have anything to do with his break-up with Petra? Surely it couldn't. That had happened a week ago.

"Why on earth would you want to marry me?"

The corners of his mouth crinkled up into a heart-stopping smile. "Lots of reasons."

So he *had* meant to ask. And at least he wasn't insulting her intelligence by claiming to love her.

Tilting her head to one side, Miranda studied him. The tantalizing thought of hardheaded Callum in love was impossible to envision. He hadn't loved Petra—even though she would've made him a perfect wife. Especially considering her father was a major shareholder in Ironstone Insurance. Callum and Petra came from the same world. Whereas Callum imagined Miranda's father to be nothing more than a thief.

And then of course with her flawless oval face, blond hair and pale blue eyes, the other woman was exquisitely beautiful. The children she and Callum would've shared would almost certainly have been blue-eyed little angels. Thinking about them caused an unexpected glass splinter of pain to pierce Miranda's heart.

Callum had admitted he'd intended to marry the beautiful blonde—he'd even bought a ring.

So why was he asking Miranda to marry him? "Name one reason."

"Your cooking is to die for."

Even though mirth bubbled up inside her, she didn't laugh as he'd clearly meant for her to do. Instead, refusing to be distracted, she gave him her most severe look and said, "This is no laughing matter. Or was your proposal meant as a joke?"

She had to know.

In response his fingertips stroked across the back of her hand, and under his touch she caught fire. Her blood fizzed and a heady excitement seized hold of her. Okay, this definitely wasn't funny. It felt like he'd branded her as his.

She shook off the ridiculous sensation. Callum Ironstone couldn't make her his merely with a stroke of his fingers!

"And if I told you that it drives me mad with lust when you don your apron? That I have a yen to seduce you wearing a tall chef's hat? Would you accuse me of joking then?"

The intensity of his hot gaze told her this was no joke.

A wickedly erotic image flashed through

her mind of Callum pinning her up against the counter in his kitchen....

She'd be fully clothed, wearing her frilliest apron and a toque. While Callum stood between her parted legs, naked and virile. His fingers dipping into a pot of rich, dark chocolate mousse then offering them to her. She licked the mousse delicately from his fingertips...he moaned...his blue eyes blazed, promising to pleasure her from head to toe before the night was out....

Good grief. Where had that come from?

A flush seared her face, scorching all the way down her body to her most private places. Her voice cracking, she said, "No one gets turned on by that getup."

"If you say so."

His cheekbones stood out under tightly drawn skin. He looked dark and dangerous and unbelievably desirable.

"Sex on its own is never a good reason for marriage," she told him fiercely, a warning to herself as much as him. The fantasy flash had disturbed her far more than she cared to admit.

"I can't think of a better reason."

Her breath died abruptly in her throat as he gazed at her with raw, unvarnished hunger.

Callum Ironstone wanted her.

For one wild moment she was tempted to flee. From him—and from her own riotous imaginings. She scanned across the restaurant, checking if the escape route was clear, and except for one waiter balancing a tray on his shoulder, it was.

She should run. Now.

If she stayed it might be too late to free herself from the power of his attraction. Callum posed a risk that she'd never anticipated.

Yet an overwhelming desire for an answer to the question she'd posed kept her in the chair, even as his hands caressed hers with slow deliberation.

He couldn't be offering marriage to get her into his bed—he'd already done that. There *had* to be more to it than this incomprehensible desire that leaped between them. And he'd already made it clear, love had nothing to do with it.

Questions buzzed around inside her head, multiplying into further questions. But before she could utter them, he bent his head closer to hers. In the candlelight she could see all the way into the bright blue eyes, to the black flecks that lurked like hazardous rocks in a deceptively calm stretch of sea.

"I think we could make a fantastic team."

"You and me? A team?" Was the man insane?

"Shh." He laid his index finger against his lips. "Hear me out."

Miranda found herself following that finger and staring at the beauty of the full lower lip that softened his strong features and gave an unexpected sensuality to the arrogantly handsome face.

His hand dropped back to rest on the tablecloth beside hers, and to her consternation Miranda was acutely aware of the inch of distance separating their fingers.

She hadn't wanted him reducing her to a quivering mass just by the stroke of his fingers, had she?

"You have a gift—one that complements my strengths," he was saying. "With your skills—"

"A gift? You mean cooking?" She jerked her head back in disbelief. "So you really do want to marry me for my cooking?"

"It's more than that. You have an ability to make people feel not only nourished, but also cherished on a level I cannot reach."

Warmth filled her at the unexpected compliment. Yet she realized it was true. She'd always cared for those close to her—her family were sure of her love. Nourish. Cherish. He'd articulated something that she'd only ever been dimly aware of in the back of her consciousness. "Thank you. That's a nice thing to say."

He shook his head. "Not nice. Absolutely true. And it's a talent I can use."

The warmth fizzled out.

"You would be able to take care of a side of my life I don't have time to deal with."

Of course. Everything was always about what he could use. What he could turn to profit. He must've been born with a calculator for a heart.

Miranda raised her glass and took a careful sip. Despite the rush of bubbles to the surface, the champagne tasted flat. A reflection of her state of mind, no doubt. She set the glass down. "You want to marry me so I can sort your business entertaining."

He didn't deny it.

What had she expected? Callum was running one hundred percent true to type.

"Gee, you must be patting yourself on the back for the wise investment you made paying for my culinary training."

His mouth compressed into a tight line. "Don't be so cynical. You'd be far more than a chef. You'd be my *wife,* for God's sake. You'd run my life."

"Mrs. Callum Ironstone. A useful wife with no identity of her own." The idea chilled her. There would be no room for nourishing or cherishing in such a life. "And what about love and romance and all the reasons people usually get married?" What about all *her* dreams and hopes?

Flags of color scorched his cheekbones and his eyes sparked. "I have every intention of sleeping with *Mrs. Ironstone,*" he said between clenched teeth. "This won't be some platonic marriage. We've already proved we're a very good fit."

Fit? It made her sound like a damn suit that he could shed when she'd outworn her use.

After a quick glance around revealed no one was looking their way, she lowered her voice and said, "I spoke of love, Callum. Not sex."

An unreadable expression flitted over his face. "Love is an emotional complication neither of us need."

"Speak for yourself. I don't see love as an emotional complication."

He gave her a superior smile. "Of course it is. Look at you—just talking about love is getting you wound up. Sex will allow you to relax, unwind." His fingertips crossed the inch of tablecloth that had become no-man's land to play along the tender skin of her inner wrist, and Miranda quivered in reaction as tingles exploded up her arm. He paused, exploring the fine lilac lines of her pulse, and the smile became reckless. "But if romance is so important to you…I can take care of that."

Despite her madly racing pulse, Miranda went down fighting. "Your idea of romance is roses and hot sex."

His hands, damn them, cradled hers with a tenderness that she knew meant nothing.

"What's wrong with that?" He truly did look puzzled. "It would be far better to keep our relationship straightforward. We both know we set each other on fire in bed—I've never experienced anything like it," he admitted with a raw honesty she had no choice but to believe. "That's why I had to end it with Petra."

He leaned closer across the table. She could smell the crisp, clean scent of him—so male with a hint of bergamot and musk underpinning it.

It would be so easy to give in—it would solve all her problems.

She wouldn't have to worry about Gianni or Mick at work. Or her family. All her financial worries would become a thing of the past in an instant. Callum would take care of everything. She'd be able to resign from The Golden Goose and she'd simply present him with Flo's debts to settle. His wealth would mean Adrian's and Flo's debts wouldn't make a dent.

Dent…

Help! He still didn't know about Adrian's accident, and she suspected Callum wouldn't be quite so sanguine about her keeping him in the dark. Yet Adrian had asked her not to tell Callum. How could she betray her brother?

Oh, this was dreadful.

A wave of shame swept her that she'd even considered accepting his proposal for such superficial reasons. She'd be using him. Marrying him for his wealth.

Hadn't he admitted that he intended to use her, too? But that was no reason to stoop to his level. When she married, it would be because she loved a man so much she didn't want to live without him.

Miranda stopped herself from sighing aloud. It was better this way. They didn't even share the same life views. And she wasn't likely to change him.

She shook her hands free from his. "I can't marry you."

"You can't?" He looked utterly surprised.

He'd expected her to say yes? But Miranda found that she had no urge to laugh at the stunned expression in his eyes. Instead a curious hollowness settled in the space beneath her heart. "I want more, Callum." *Much more.*

"I see."

But she doubted he did. And it was too hard to explain.

Putting her elbows on the table, she dropped her face into the cup of her hands, feeling utterly wretched.

The touch of a finger under her chin caused her to lift her head. It was only the pad of his index finger yet she was aware of his touch through her whole body.

When she met his eyes, she could read little there. But then he was hardly the kind of man a woman could read like a glossy gossip rag.

And that enigmatic quality was part of what drew her to him again and again even though she knew it was downright self-destructive.

"Look, I really do need your help."

"What help?" she asked with more than a little suspicion. After all, he was an Ironstone.

"Our family always spends Christmas at Fairwinds."

At the height of her hatred for Callum, she'd pored over *Country Life* images of Fairwinds, the Ironstones' country retreat set on Lake Windermere's bank in the Lake District. A long tree-lined lane cutting through a grassy park, a forecourt edged with neatly clipped box hedging, and a flight of stone stairs leading up to the imposing house with its mullioned windows and a steep jagged roofline. The photos had oozed old wealth and gracious living.

And she'd raged against how unfair life was.

Miranda shook herself free of the memory. "Why are you telling me this?"

"I'd like you to spend Christmas with us," he said, "as my partner for the weekend."

Miranda sucked in a breath.

"It's my mother's birthday," he continued, "the day after Christmas. We're planning to throw her a surprise birthday party—and Gordon and Petra have already been invited."

Callum didn't need to add that he'd originally planned to take Petra along to his mother's birthday as his fiancée. That his break-up with the blonde had caused a horrible complication. It was written all over his discomfited face. And that knowledge caused an unexpected wash of bittersweet sensation to engulf Miranda.

"You're asking me to come along and *protect* you?"

Heavens, men could be so *obtuse.*

"Something like that." The barely imperceptible tension that had been coiled within him eased a little, and his eyes smiled into hers. "You could take over working the kitchen on the weekend. I'd make it worth your while."

Miranda itched to slap him.

"My mother always goes to a great deal of trouble over the festive season—works herself half to death, which makes us all feel guilty. This year she turns sixty." His expression held a tenderness she'd never seen. "We want to spoil her rotten. We'd planned to get some help with the Christmas preparations, but we've all been involved with the merger and no one's gotten around to organizing it. Neglectful sons, aren't we?"

There was something inherently sweet about the thought of four grown men—five if you counted his father—coming up with such an idea. It made her turn to marshmallow.

"We'd even pay you—top rates, given that it will be over the Christmas weekend."

For a moment she thought of her family. She'd never spent Christmas away from them. But how could she possibly resist? The commission Callum was dangling in front of her would enable her to put something toward the deposit Adrian wanted for the pre-owned BMW he'd already agreed to buy from a friend before the expense of the accident—and maybe even buy her mother the new microwave she desperately wanted. And she had to admit to a yearning to see the home in the country that he'd spoken of with such affection.

The only thing that concerned her about his request was Petra. How did the other woman feel about Callum? Miranda suspected Petra would be wounded to be faced with her supposed successor. It made her feel uncomfortable.

Callum must have seen her hesitation because he asked, "Will you come?", giving her a charmingly lopsided smile. "Will you make my mother's life, my life—all our lives—so much easier?"

Faced with his love for his mother, how could she refuse? He cared for his mother, loved her. That was beyond doubt. She was discovering a side of Callum she'd never seen before.

Or had she?

Even though he barely knew Flo, he'd taken care of her since her husband's death. More than Miranda had ever realized. He'd misjudged her father with tragic results...but he hadn't walked away and abandoned them. Anonymously he'd tried to make amends in the best way he could—by making sure she and her brother received a top-class education, and by looking after the widow of the man he'd wronged.

Perhaps it was time for her to let up on him a little. He'd done wrong, but he'd clearly regretted the consequences his actions had produced.

She'd intended to throw all his money back in his face once she scrimped it together. Yet here was something he was asking her to do, something that could ease her burden of the debt.

Their food arrived before she could answer, the two waiters whipping off the silver covers of the plates with a flourish.

After she'd made the expected noises of approval, they departed. And, drawing a deep breath, Miranda said, "I think it's a lovely gesture. Your mother will adore a birthday celebration. Of course I'll come."

"Toothbrush. Shampoo. Perfume."

Miranda packed the final items into her toiletry

holdall and tossed it into her overnight bag. Then, crumpling up her list, she dropped it into the bin beneath her dressing table.

"You're all packed?"

She hadn't heard her mother come in. Miranda turned her head to smile at Flo. "Only my cooking stuff left to pack—at least Callum's Daimler has plenty of space. I'm going to miss you and Adrian, Mum."

"You'll be back after the weekend on Boxing Day." Flo patted her arm. "Not that long."

But it would be over Christmas. "With Christmas falling on Friday this year, Boxing Day seems so far away."

Flo gave her a kiss on the cheek. "I'll keep you some Christmas pudding, darling."

"That would be lovely." Her mother made the best Christmas pudding in the whole world.

"Adrian's already up. Should we open our presents before you go?"

Miranda studied Flo. "Wouldn't you prefer to wait until Christmas tomorrow?"

"It will be so strange without you. Let me see what Adrian wants to do."

Flo waltzed out, and Miranda gathered up the modest gifts she'd bought for her mother and Adrian, before making her way to the small lounge.

Adrian and Flo were already waiting, Flo all but dancing with excitement as she pushed a package into Miranda's hands. "We're doing it now. Save mine until last."

Miranda laughed. "I will, I will." She handed Adrian the bottle of aftershave she'd bought him—one she knew he liked. "This is yours. When I get paid for this weekend's work, I'll give you a check to put toward the BMW—that way your friend will at least continue to hold it for you. I'd like to get Mum a microwave, too."

Adrian's face lit up. "Thanks, sis. That's awesome. One day I'll repay everything you've done for me."

Miranda felt a niggle of misgiving. "Pay me back? You don't need to. It's a gift."

Her brother looked uncomfortable. "One you can't afford—not if you want to get out of The Golden Goose."

Had she become so tight about money that her brother couldn't accept a gift from her anymore? It reminded her of her own determination to pay Callum back come hell or high water.

But Adrian was family. It was different.

Before she could say anything more, he handed her a flat parcel. "It's a boring gift. But I think you'll enjoy it."

It was a book by a chef she admired. She hugged him, then she settled down and tore the wrapping from the package her mother had given her. Her fingers peeled back the paper to reveal a red woolen scarf. She drew it out. It was as soft as the silk she'd collected from the silkworms she'd reared as a child, the wool fine and warm against her fingertips.

How much had it cost?

She bit back the question. "It's beautiful. Thanks, Mum."

Flo's eyes glowed with happiness. "Take it with you. That color does marvelous things for your skin. I knew it was yours the moment I spotted it. And here's something else."

A second, much larger, package landed in her lap.

"Mum, you didn't need to..." Her voice trailed away as she saw the ivory trench coat that lay inside.

"They're very in this season, darling."

Miranda felt as if she'd been turned to stone. She stared at the coat. But instead of seeing a garment, all she could see were bills.

Unpaid bills.

"Mother..." She looked up. "Please don't tell me that you've extended your credit further. Tell me you won a lottery. Anything. Just not more debt."

The happiness on her mother's face subsided. "Oh, Miranda, don't spoil it."

Beside her mother, Adrian fidgeted.

"We can't afford this, Flo."

She'd have to face Callum, tell him that her

mother was still using his name. Then she'd have to pay him back. The debt stretched ahead of her like an unscaleable mountain. "Oh, Mum."

"Don't 'Oh, Mum' me." Her mother stood up abruptly. "You're not the only one allowed to give nice presents."

"What do you mean?"

"You just promised Adrian you'd help him with the deposit on his car—and possibly buy me the new model microwave I've been wanting. But we're not allowed to give you anything nice?"

Adrian looked like he wished he was far away.

"It's not the size—or the expense—of the present that counts. It never has been." Miranda folded the wrappings over the coat. "You need to take this back. Get the account credited."

Her mother's shoulders sagged. "But you'll keep the scarf?"

She took in her mother's dejection. With an inward sigh Miranda conceded, "Yes, I will."

Flo perked up instantly. "And wear it this weekend. That red lipstick of yours will match it perfectly."

Miranda crossed over to her mother and hugged her. Flo stood quietly in the circle of her arms, and Miranda noticed that her mother had become as fragile as a butterfly; she was thinner than she'd ever been. "I love you, Mum."

How she wished that things were different. For Flo to be more reasonable. For her father to be here.

Ah, what did it help to wish for the impossible?

Her father wasn't coming back.

And she was spending the weekend with the man who had caused his death. A man who'd asked her to be his wife.

What a traitor she'd become.

Eight

Everything was packed and ready to take to Fairwinds. There was some baking that with Flo's help Miranda had prepared in advance, a selection of herbs and spices that she never traveled without—and extras that she intended to gift to the family—as well as a plethora of laborsaving devices and utensils.

Unfortunately it had been raining since they'd opened presents, making it impossible for her to stack it all outside, and now Callum was due to collect her.

Deciding she had to get moving, regardless of

the weather, she kissed her mother goodbye and moved to hug Adrian.

He pecked her on the cheek. "I'll give you a hand with all your junk." Picking up her overnight bag, he held the front door open for her. "I'll make a second trip for the bigger boxes."

Miranda smiled her thanks up to him. "What would I do without you?" she said teasingly, then realized it was true—she loved her brother, would do whatever she could to protect him.

Outside the rain had eased off. Droplets dripped from the eaves, while the wind whistled through the bare branches of the lone potted silver birch.

"Look after Mum," she told her brother on the step.

Adrian set down her bag. "I will."

He was back in a jiffy with her boxes and stacked them at the bottom of the steps beside her luggage. "It's going to snow again," he said, studying the sky.

"Maybe." Miranda squinted at the heavy clouds overhead. "Remember how we used to make snowmen in winter? With an old pair of Dad's gumboots? Once we borrowed Mum's pink scarf and she was so cross."

Adrian chuckled beside her. "Remember the time you pulled my carrot nose out and gave it to Troubadour? We had such a snowball fight after that."

"You stole the horse's carrot. And anyway, you started it. You put a handful of snow down my shirt." Miranda grimaced. "You hooligan."

"And you clobbered me with your riding crop, so I hit you back."

"And then Dad came and gave you a lecture about how boys should behave with honor always." A lump thickened her throat. "I'd forgotten about that. We were a right royal pair of brats sometimes."

Adrian stopped laughing. "Miranda—"

His eyes were full of turbulence, and her heart sank. "What's wrong?"

"I'm sorry to have to add this to everything, sis."

Oh, no. What had her talk of honor provoked? "What? What's happened now?"

Adrian flinched.

She tried to temper her impatience. "Callum will be here any minute. Tell me."

"The panel beater who fixed the car—"

"What did he do wrong?" That was the last thing they needed. Had the car been shoddily repaired. Or worse?

"Nothing—he fixed it. The car's been back at work for days—otherwise it would've been missed."

"Then what's the problem?"

"He's threatening to tell my supervisor I borrowed the car without permission unless…"

"Unless what?"

"Unless I pay him more money."

She stared at her brother aghast. "This man's blackmailing you?"

"He says if I pay him, he'll stay quiet."

"You're actually considering paying this lowlife hush money?"

Adrian shrugged. "I don't exactly have a choice."

"And where *exactly*—" she said with emphasis

"—is the money going to come from? Please tell me you're not going to rob a bank—that would hardly be honorable."

He recoiled at her sarcasm, then shot her a quick look. "I thought—"

Miranda shook her head and said grimly, "No, you can unthink that idea right now. I'm not giving you the money. Not even as a loan. If you pay him once, it will never end."

"So what am I supposed to do?" Adrian had gone pale beneath his freckles.

"Report him to the police. But first come clean to Callum about what you did—it's hardly as bad as extortion."

Adrian looked horrified. "I can't."

"You must." At the glimpse of ghostly gray in her peripheral vision she added flatly, "He's here. Why don't you talk to him now?"

The sight of Callum's Daimler pulling up at the curb caused Adrian to blanch further. "Please, sis, I'm begging you—don't tell him."

"He should know."

His eyes darted around. "Not now. Not yet. I

need time to think about what I'm going to say—and I really should be going to work."

His eyes pleaded with her.

After a moment, Miranda caved in. "Okay, but you *must* tell him—otherwise you'll leave me no choice but to do it myself."

She shuddered at the thought of it.

"As soon as you get back," he promised, giving her a sick smile. "I don't want to spend Christmas in jail while you try to arrange bail."

"It won't come to that." At least she hoped not. But she still shivered as Callum got out of the car and came round to greet her.

Her brother acknowledged Callum with none of his usual confidence and quickly sidled away, saying, "Drive carefully, and have a merry Christmas both of you."

Despite the fact that there had been heavy snows a few days earlier, the roads were clear and they were making good time.

Callum glanced over at the woman beside him. Apart from a few monosyllabic answers,

Miranda hadn't spoken much in the past three hours. After trying to engage her in conversation a couple of times, he'd shrugged and flooded the car with music, negating the need for conversation.

Right now she was scribbling in a notebook, a frown of concentration wrinkling her brow.

"Don't worry, everything will go like clock-work."

"I'm not worried." But the way she gnawed the end of her pencil refuted the statement. And so did the closed, withdrawn expression that had been etched on her face since he'd collected her earlier.

"Try to relax, my family won't bite."

"If you say so."

Callum fell silent.

She must be nervous. That would explain her behavior. They'd spoken several times over the past few days. At first she'd made panicked calls to him about logistics, but each time they'd spoken, she'd sounded more and more like the Miranda he knew. Smart. Confident. Totally together. After consultation with his brothers, and with his parents' housekeeper, he'd approved all the menus she'd produced—and given her carte blanche to buy whatever she needed.

With the housekeeper's help, Miranda had decided to employ three women from the local village to help with the birthday party, and to hire the majority of the crockery and cutlery needed from a firm in Ambleside. Much of the produce would come from local suppliers, too, which she'd already organized.

As late as last night, there'd been no problem. So why was she so withdrawn and tense now?

Or was he imagining problems where none existed? Callum shrugged his concern off. It could be that Miranda simply wasn't a morning person—he'd teased her about that before. Or maybe she needed sustenance.

So fifteen minutes later he pulled off the M6 and headed for an inn set well back from the main road.

She looked up with surprise as he turned into the car park. "Where are we?"

He gestured to a large sign in front of the inn. "The Rose and Thorn."

She groaned. "That much is evident—I can see the sign."

His mouth twitched as he sensed her rolling her eyes.

Switching off the motor, he unclipped his seat belt. "I often break the journey here. They serve a good breakfast." He went round to her side and opened her door. "If you don't want breakfast, my mother swears by their cream teas."

She hesitated.

"Come on." Miranda was shivering as the cold air drifted into the warmth of the Daimler. "There's a warm fire inside," he coaxed as she drew her red scarf more tightly around her neck and emerged from the car in a flurry of denim and a bright red woolen coat.

Inside the dining room, the low wooden beams and a fire in the hearth gave the inn a welcoming ambience. Once a plump, smiling woman had taken their orders, Callum watched Miranda's gaze settle on a large

Christmas tree in the corner. Her shoulders sagged imperceptibly.

"What's the matter?" he asked.

Miranda shook her head.

"Don't fob me off." He waited, but she still said nothing, though shadows lingered in her eyes. "This is me, Callum. When have you ever not been able to tell me exactly what you think?"

She gestured to the Christmas tree. "This will be the first time I haven't been with my family for Christmas." She slanted him a glance from under long, dark lashes and the expression in her melting eyes caught at something deep in his chest. "Nothing you can do about that."

He exhaled in relief. "That's all?"

"All? What do you mean 'all'?" The fire was back in her eyes. "No one is as important to me as Mum and Adrian. Since Dad died we've always roasted a Cornish hen—a turkey is too big for the three of us—and prepared all the trimmings. And this year I won't be there."

Callum cursed silently as he filled in the

unspoken blanks. There probably hadn't been sufficient money for a turkey after her father's death. Remorse tugged at him that Miranda would be missing out on precious time with her family because of him.

Because he was prepared to go to any lengths to get her back in his bed.

God, he'd been selfish. If she ever learned how he'd manipulated her, she would be furious. So she had better never learn the truth.

The egg and bacon pie they'd both ordered from the special-of-the-day board arrived, distracting them both for a few minutes.

She continued with a wan smile. "Next year Adrian will probably be gone—out making his own life."

"That happened for a while with my family. It's part of growing up. But Adrian will return to the fold." He thought of his own family. "These days all my brothers go home for Christmas each year. It's rare that one of us doesn't make it."

"Four boys! Your poor mother. It couldn't have been easy. Isn't Hunter your stepbrother?"

At the glint of curiosity in her eyes, he explained, "Hunter and Jack are my half brothers. Dad married Mother after his first wife died. He already had Hunter and Jack. Then he and Mother had Fraser and me."

"I knew you were the youngest, but I wasn't sure who were your real brothers—you all seem so close."

"We are close. Hunter and Jack are every bit as much my brothers as Fraser is. And Dad had a busy job so most of the task of bringing us up landed on Mum." He waited for Miranda to make a comment about how privileged they all were, but she didn't. "Once Dad retired, Mother was very relieved. She's always wanted to live in the country—although I don't think she expected it to be quite so wet in winter."

Miranda's eyes were full of longing. "I can understand that—I wouldn't care about the wet though."

She'd grown up in the country, he knew. "You miss it, don't you?"

"I have fond memories of living there. Just

the—" she broke off "—the ending wasn't so nice."

Callum knew her home had been auctioned off after her father's suicide—along with most of the furniture and valuables. He'd done what he'd could to help patch up the shambles of her parents' finances but it hadn't been enough.

"I think one of the worst things was saying goodbye to Troubadour."

"Troubadour?"

"My horse. I'd had him since I was thirteen and he was rising three. I loved that horse."

Another loss.

Her father. Her home. Her horse.

Everything she'd loved. Everything dear and familiar to her. Gone.

Callum fell silent and dug into the bacon and egg pie as if he was waging a battle.

"Look, I don't know how we got into such distressing topics." She made a dismissive gesture with her hand. "It's too depressing—especially so near to Christmas."

He laid down his knife and fork. "I think we

do need to talk about it," he said gently. He wanted to reach out and touch the hands he suspected would be ice-cold despite the warmth of the inn's fire.

"I'd rather not." She inhaled audibly, and gave him a very fake and, to his mind, a very brave smile. "It's not practical to live in the country. London is where the work is."

Her deliberate changing of the subject warned Callum that the past still affected her deeply.

Would she ever be able to let it go?

A restless edginess shook him. He faced the fact that she might never do so. And that would leave them forever estranged. The realization was akin to looking down into a long, dark tunnel, one without a glimpse of day at the other side.

He wasn't ready to exist in perpetual darkness. He'd find a way to see the sunlight on the other side. Because the notion of never holding her again, never making love to her, was one he wasn't ready to accept.

It left him with no choice. She was going to

hate him for reopening the wounds, but if he didn't, he might as well kiss any chance of having her back in his bed goodbye now. Without resolving the past, they had no future.

However, now was probably not the best time to address it. Taking the conversational olive branch she'd offered, he gestured around. "The big money might be in London, but surely there are enough places like this where you could have the country lifestyle you want?"

"Maybe, but I never wanted to be an inn-keeper—" she pulled a face that he found rather endearing "—or a café owner. I'd be perfectly happy catering for an array of the rich and famous."

He laughed but his eyes remained fixed on her. "Is that what you really want?"

Her lips firmed. "What I really want isn't possible, so I live with what is."

She wanted her father back. "Look, about your father—"

"You've already apologized. Let's leave it there." She glanced down, her lashes forming dark shadows against her creamy skin, and her body had gone very still.

Callum couldn't leave it—it pervaded their whole relationship.

Three years ago he'd been appointed to the board as financial director after returning from five years of working in Australia. He'd worked all hours, day and night, to get on top of the chaos after his predecessor—a good friend of his father's—had resigned with a colon cancer scare. The cruel whispers of nepotism had infuriated Callum—particularly as he didn't want to hurt his father's friend with the truth.

Callum had been unknown and unproven, and that had fueled his fierce desperation to prove to his brothers, to the management team and to the skeptical naysayers that he could do the task his father had set upon him.

He'd probably gone over the top.

He'd certainly adopted a take-no-prisoners management style.

How best to explain the climate against which

his actions had played out? Whatever he said was going to sound like justification for his arrogance.

He chose his words carefully. "If I could have that time of my life over again, I would have handled things differently."

Miranda met his gaze. "*Handled things differently? You mean you would've done a decent job of investigating before you issued a statement to the press that damaged a good and honorable man, before you called the police in to arrest my father?*" The eyes that had seduced him were full of pain. "The humiliation of that was what killed him."

"Wait a moment!" He leaned forward. "Even if no statement had been made to the press, your father would still have been arrested—just perhaps not so publicly."

Her expression grew closed, shutting out anything he could say. "My father didn't steal anything from your company," she bit out.

She still believed her father had done nothing wrong. Callum sighed. "Miranda, you need to face the truth."

"It's *not* the truth. Let's just agree to disagree." She picked up her bag and rose to her feet.

God, but this woman was stubborn!

He snagged her elbow as she tried to force her way past his chair and pulled her to him. Ignoring the startled looks from the only other couple in the dining room, two gray-haired women, he murmured close to her face, "Your parents were living way beyond their means. I can only assume your father meant to pay back the money he took."

She tossed the gold, tousled hair that always gave him bedroom fantasies. The gesture made him want to haul her into his arms. He wasn't sure what he'd do next—shake some sense into her…or kiss her stupid.

"He never took it—he left us letters telling us that."

"Letters?"

Callum had never heard anything about any letters.

"Before he shut himself up in the garage and gassed himself, he wrote letters to me and Adrian and Mum telling us that he loved us. He said he could *never* have done such a thing—that he'd been convincingly framed for his predecessor's mistakes, and that the humiliation of living with it was too much for him. He apologized for being weak."

Her eyes filled with tears, but her pain and anger glittered through the moisture. "The whole charge was a fiction to cover administrative blunders from the financial department. You know that—you've already said you were sorry for framing him."

"No!" Jeez, how had this happened? He couldn't let her labor under such a misunderstanding. "I never said that. I was apologizing for making your father's shame so public—I didn't need to have been quite so gung ho, but my appointment was still fresh and I thought I needed to stamp my authority. I've never said his arrest was unjust. I believe people should be held accountable for their actions—"

But Miranda pulled her arm free. "I'm not listening to this garbage. You're lying! I'll wait for you at the car."

* * *

By the time Callum stalked out of the Rose and Thorn fifteen minutes later, Miranda's teeth were chattering.

She supposed it served her right. She could've waited in the warm hallway, but she'd been so angry, all she'd wanted was to get out of the space Callum occupied. She'd needed to breathe the clean, crisp air outside to cool down.

Without glancing in her direction, he pointed the key fob at the car and the doors unlocked. She scuttled in and Callum climbed in beside her.

When he didn't start the car, she swiveled her head to see what the holdup was. And nearly wilted under the blast of his blue gaze.

He said softly, with lethal contempt, "I'm going to say this once more and never again. I would never have a man I believed to be innocent arrested."

Maybe Callum didn't know the full extent of it. "The evidence was falsified. He was framed."

"The written admission from your father was not falsified."

The quiet menace of his statement silenced Miranda like nothing else could have.

"And no one tampered with the evidence he produced that showed what he'd done with the money he'd misappropriated."

Her lips parted, but the shock of what he was telling her had frozen her vocal cords. At last she stuttered, "That's a lie." *It had to be.*

A muscle flexed high in his cheek but no emotion crossed his face. "You must believe what you will."

Bile burned bitterly in the back of her throat as her stomach clenched in fear. She'd been lied to before. In the past few months, her mother and brother had both lied to her, but Callum never had. She'd even believed the lie her mother had been spinning for years about the life insurance policy paying out. Callum had debunked that myth. And he'd been telling the truth.

"You're lying," she said without hope.

He looked pained—as if he was hurting.

Miranda leaned her head back against the head rest and closed her eyes, shutting him out. A few seconds later the car started, and soon they were back on the main road.

She pretended to sleep, but her mind ticked over.

Callum was nothing if not honest. Even when he'd asked her to marry him, he'd never iced what was essentially a practical request—albeit garnished with lashings of sex—into a romantically pretty proposal.

What if he was telling the truth this time, too?

The hurt that seized her was unbearable. Her father wouldn't have lied to her. It was important to believe that, to keep faith lest her whole world come tumbling down around her like a pack of fraudster's cards.

Yet even while she clutched onto that belief, deep within her most secret heart, something withered.

Near the town of Windermere, they turned off onto a road with breathtaking views of the lake dotted with sailing craft tied up for winter.

Another turn took them into a narrow lane flanked with low stone walls while snow-covered fields lay beyond.

Their speed had slowed, and Miranda knew they must be approaching their final destination.

Now that they were nearly there, Miranda wished she hadn't let Adrian's latest bombshell depress her, since it was that mood that had gotten her into the bridge-burning fight with Callum. There were a thousand questions she wanted to ask as he nosed the Daimler through a set of imposing wrought-iron gates and onto a drive that wound through a park.

She sat up, squinting against the bright light. The snow, the absence of livestock, the leafless trees with their bare crisscrossing branches all gave the landscape a bleak, monochromatic beauty.

Loneliness swept her.

Huddling down, she pulled the scarf Flo had given her for Christmas tighter around her neck.

She already missed the cramped terrace house

and the merry music Flo played in the evenings. She longed for the funny, bent Christmas tree Adrian had salvaged after a Boxing Day party a couple of years ago.

Why the hell had she agreed to come? Because of an inexplicable yearning to see the place Callum called home. And, to a lesser extent, for the cash incentive he'd offered.

Because they needed the money.

Miranda gave a silent sigh. It always came back to money. A predicament *he* had put her family into. If she didn't maintain that belief, she might go mad. And while she wouldn't accept his charity, she was going to use every commission, every lead he offered, to get herself out of this financial quagmire.

At least she hadn't given in to her urge to unload the burden of Adrian being blackmailed. Judging by Callum's black-and-white statement about accountability, he would expect Adrian to face charges.

Callum was a rigid autocrat who gave no quarter. There was no doubt that he would have her brother convicted of using the car without permission.

Adrian's concern about spending Christmas in jail was too real to dismiss.

Nine

They rounded a bend and unexpectedly Fairwinds rose up against the sky ahead of them. Fingers of winter sunlight pressed through the cloud to caress the rugged blocks of hewn stone, and the mullioned windows winked in the brightening light.

"It's exquisite," Miranda breathed softly. The house was more beautiful than the spread in *Country Life* had promised.

"Every time I come home, it takes my breath away." Callum's voice was full of pride.

The Daimler rolled to a stop in the cobbled

forecourt. Instantly the heavy wooden front door swung open, and a crowd poured down the stone stairs behind two black, barking Labradors.

Before Callum could come round to her door, Miranda was already out of the car.

Callum reached the dogs first. "Mojo, Moxie, be quiet!"

The pair of dogs stopped barking and came forward to sniff Miranda. She stood still, giving them a chance to become accustomed to her scent.

"Don't be afraid. They don't bite." A woman with an elegant silver-gray bob smiled warmly at her. "I'm Pauline, Callum's mother."

The rest of the group separated themselves into his father, Robin; two of Callum's brothers, Fraser and Jack; Jack's girlfriend, Lindsey; and the housekeeper.

Once Miranda had gotten everyone's names sorted out and their luggage had been brought in, Pauline showed her upstairs to a lovely guest bedroom decorated in shades of pale blue and lilac with views over the home paddocks to the park beyond.

"There are towels as well as a range of toiletries in the en suite if you'd like to freshen up." Pauline opened a door. "If you need anything more just sing out. With the exception of Hunter, who's coming later, the whole family is here now. I'm so pleased you came with Callum. Hunter's also bringing a girl he's recently met."

Of course Pauline didn't know that more guests would be arriving on Saturday for her surprise birthday party.

It discomfited Miranda to realize that Pauline truly believed she was Callum's girlfriend. What she had thought a deception only for the benefit of the Harrises was clearly not the case. All the brothers seemed to be bringing dates home for Christmas.

Except apparently for Fraser, which prompted her to say, "I don't remember meeting Fraser's girlfriend."

"He didn't bring one. There doesn't seem to be

anyone special in his life right now—or at least not one he's telling his mother about." Pauline smiled at her. "My sons keep us in the dark. We'd actually thought Callum was about to—"

The older woman looked suddenly flustered. "What am I saying? I talk too much."

So Callum's parents had known about Petra—that Callum was going to propose to her.

Before Miranda could say anything, Pauline said, "I suppose you'll think I'm a nosy mother when I say this, but I hope you don't mind that I put you in separate rooms. I'm still a little old-fashioned that way. I like to know a couple is committed to each other before they fall into bed together. My upbringing," she explained.

Miranda felt herself flush hectically. What would this sweet woman think if she had any idea of the wild no-strings night Miranda had spent with her youngest son? There'd been no thought about commitment, only stark pleasure on the spur of the moment. She'd hated Callum—but he'd ignited a fierce blaze in her that had scorched them both without thought of tomorrow.

For sure his mother wouldn't approve.

Although Miranda feared she could hardly claim to hate Callum any longer. "Callum and I are still getting to know each other," she said, before her mother imagined the peal of wedding bells. "Our connection started with business."

Connection? What a word to choose. She groaned inwardly at the image it conjured up.

"And Callum said you're a chef?"

Miranda nodded. "I'm helping with tomorrow's catering." While Callum's mother was still in the dark about the birthday party planned for Saturday, the brothers had told her that Miranda would be preparing Christmas lunch to explain her calls to Millie, the housekeeper, and the tons of supplies she'd brought. Millie had already been given Christmas Day off.

"Thank you. It will be wonderful to have you here for Christmas, Miranda."

Miranda smiled uncomfortably at Pauline's warm words, all too conscious that she'd come to Fairwinds under false pretenses.

* * *

Under the guise of playing Monopoly, Miranda spent the next two hours closeted in the study downstairs with Callum, Fraser, Jack and Lindsey, coordinating the arrangements for Pauline's party. Three women would be coming up from the village to help with the preparation, do all the serving and clean up afterward.

Robin had been co-opted to keep Pauline occupied, but Pauline still managed to wander in from time to time to check whether they needed anything—causing Miranda to hastily cover her notes while everyone else frantically shuffled Monopoly money and moved houses around the board that was spread out on the card table.

When Hunter arrived with a tall redhead he introduced as Anna, he handed Callum a large, white envelope. "The documents you requested."

A look passed between the two brothers. Miranda tensed. What was going on? A shiver feathered down her spine.

The meeting broke up when Pauline came to

remind them that they would need to eat soon to give enough time to make the Christmas Eve carols in the nearby village. Everyone dived for the doors to ready themselves for dinner, but Callum caught Miranda's arm, restraining her from following the others.

"I have something for you." He handed her the envelope Hunter had brought. "I called Hunter from the inn and asked him to bring this."

She knew from the set of his jaw she wouldn't like whatever that envelope contained.

"Open it."

For a brief second she contemplated refusing and shoving it back at him, unopened. But curiosity got the better of her.

She lifted the flap and drew out the sheaf of papers stapled in the top corner. Her heartbeat accelerated. "What is this?"

"It's a copy of your father's confession—the original is in the police file. He signed it. I know I said earlier I wouldn't raise this again, but it's clear we've been talking at cross-purposes for some time."

No triumph glowed on Callum's face in the deathly silence that followed. Instead deep lines of concern cut into his forehead.

Miranda dropped into the chair beside the table where they'd plotted his mother's surprise. All the lighthearted camaraderie of earlier had evaporated, leaving her drained.

She was suddenly quite sure she didn't want to read the confession.

But she knew she had no choice. Not after the accusations she'd flung at Callum almost three years ago. Not after her hostility and resentment over the past few weeks.

It hurt unbearably to read of her father's desperation. Of his admission of stealing—

"One million pounds!" Shocked, her eyes flew to Callum's. *"How?"*

"By a false claim on a bogus life policy."

She bit back a stream of questions. Drawn inexorably back, she read the confession through to the end, her heart clenching when she reached her father's familiar signature at the end of the document.

Had he written that sweet, loving note absolving himself of all responsibility after this stark admission of his guilt?

She'd never know.

"In case you think that's a forgery—the police have the original along with a certificate of identification. Once your father died, they dropped the criminal charges against him—and the company chose not to pursue civil action against your father's estate after the bulk of the funds were recovered."

The slim thread of hope that Callum had been mistaken or misinformed snapped. The charges against her father had never been unfair or trumped up. And Callum was clearly in no way responsible for her father's death. "Where did you find the money?"

"From accounts in your father's name."

Callum stood a few feet away, arms folded, offering none of the support she'd become accustomed to. And Miranda knew she deserved none. The distance between them yawned wider than it had ever been.

She said nothing. There was nothing to say.

"And before you point out the confession could have been forced, the bank manager identified your father as the person who'd opened an account in the name of the fictitious deceased. When the large deposit arrived, he became suspicious. And when he discovered that your father's name—the only contact telephone number on the account—didn't match the account holder, he notified the bank's fraud department. His statement was corroborated by video footage showing Thomas entering the bank on the date that the fictitious account was opened." Callum related the facts in a remote tone that gave no comfort. "There are other equally damning statements on file. No way such a body of evidence could be falsified."

Her father was guilty.

For years, hatred for Callum had sustained her, given her someone to blame for the hopeless sense of loss and disorientation after her father's death. The unanswerable questions that had haunted her.

Why, Dad? Why kill yourself? Why not endure it and clear your name?

Now she knew. Her father couldn't clear his name. And he hadn't been able to face up to what he'd done. Hadn't been able to face a prison term.

She pushed the pages back into the envelope, feeling as if she'd opened Pandora's box. Her life would never be the same again. "He had a family. A home. A great job. Why would he have done such a thing?"

"Thomas lived to a certain standard of living and he wanted to maintain that. He told me once that his wife was a real lady and he was her humble servant, that he would always give her everything she wanted."

"I remember him saying that, too." She'd thought it wildly romantic. "But I wouldn't have wanted him to commit fraud for our family to have such a lifestyle. We could've sold our house, found a cottage. I could have hired Troubadour out to the local riding school. There were so many expenses we could have saved." *If he'd only told us.*

But it was true, Flo had always liked to maintain a certain lifestyle. With her husband gone, Flo had simply moved on to make free with Callum's largesse.

"That reminds me—you never did stop Mum's accounts, did you?"

He shook his head.

"She's been running them up again with Christmas spending." Miranda sighed. "We're going to have to pay that amount back to you." Perhaps she should just become his hostess indefinitely without pay to offset the debts her family owed him, she thought blackly. And Flo would simply keep running them up. She would never be free of Callum.

When she got back to London, she was going to have to take Flo in hand.

"You can't take responsibility for what Flo owes."

"She's my mother."

His brows jerked together. "Flo is an adult."

"I'm not sure she's ever been treated like an adult in her life."

The housekeeper popped her head around the doorjamb. "Sorry to interrupt, but dinner is served."

"Give us a few minutes to clean up and we'll be there." Callum's frown had vanished abruptly.

When the housekeeper had gone, he took two steps closer.

Feeling unaccountably nervous, Miranda gestured with the envelope between them. "I'll run upstairs and put this away."

"Miranda…" A strange, almost hesitant expression flitted across his face. "I hope we can start afresh—put the past behind us."

The veil had been ripped off what she had believed for years, revealing a truth so sordid it had shaken her to the roots of her self. "I hope so, too. But I need time to absorb this. I don't even know if I can ever be the same person I was this morning. My whole life has shifted."

The winter night air was crisp and cold.

Miranda closed the door of the Daimler behind her and hitched her scarf more snugly around her neck as she gazed around. After the shock of reading her father's confession earlier, she'd expected the world to look different.

But it didn't. It was still winter. That hadn't changed. Even though her world had tipped upside down around her, the seasons had at least remained constant.

Only she had changed.

Wrapped up in a warm coat and her new scarf, Miranda trudged through the snowy sludge beside Callum, past homes lit with merry Christmas lights, to a village green beside a little church.

She took a proffered song sheet with small smile of thanks before hurrying to catch up with Callum. In the glow of the flickering tree lights, they found his family near the village Christmas tree, where a brass band had set up. Minutes later the bells in the church tower pealed out, heralding the arrival of the carolers.

The crowd pressed closer and as the band launched into an overture, a tall man moved in front of them, blocking Miranda's view.

Callum's hand pressed against the small of her back, guiding her to a place where her view was unobstructed. "Better?"

"Much." She threw him a quicksilver smile over her shoulder. "Thank you."

In the light of the lampposts she watched his gaze soften. She'd hated the sense of alienation between them. The first notes of "We Three Kings" struck up and she turned to watch the carolers, acutely conscious of Callum's bulk behind her.

As more people arrived, the crush shifted forward and he pressed up against her. The heavy warmth of his body crept into hers and a delicious, unfamiliar contentment stole through her.

He said something she couldn't hear.

"What?" She tipped her head back and the top of her head brushed his chin.

"Your hair smells of vanilla and cinnamon," he said into her ear. "It's a heady fragrance."

The heat of his breath in the whorls of her ear caused tingles to ripple along her spine. Her awareness of him, never long absent, rocketed up.

"Just ordinary shampoo," she said, tilting her head so she could see his face.

"There's nothing ordinary about you," he said.

The moment stretched. Tension built within her as their eyes held. Her breathing quickened.

She forced herself to look away.

No.

She didn't want this.

Not now. Not with Callum.

Even though it felt so right. Even though she'd accepted he wasn't to blame for her father's suicide, there was too much history between them. An affair with him would only bring un-happiness—especially once he found out that while he'd always been brutally truthful, she'd been less honest.

She shivered, and a wave of ever-present lone-liness swamped her.

Callum wrapped his arms around her from behind and pulled her to rest against the length of his body. "I'll keep you warm."

She let herself sag into the safe refuge of his arms. It felt strangely like coming home.

A dangerous dream.

The band was playing "Silent Night." All around, Miranda was aware of couples, young and old, of families, and the joy of Christmas Eve surrounding them.

She wanted that joy. That love. It came to her in a moment of clarity that she'd been a fool to turn down Callum's proposal.

If she'd agreed to marry him, it all would have been hers—companionship, great sex and a life with a man who did his best to consider her and solve all her problems.

"Tomorrow morning, I'll take you for a walk in the snow. There won't be time for a ride, but the horses will be out in the field in the morning and you can meet them."

How could she have been so dense?

While she'd been intent on hating him, fighting him, she'd been falling in love with Callum. How she wished…

Then reality kicked in. Callum would never *love* her. He might desire her with fierce passion, but that wasn't love. He'd told her point-blank he didn't want the emotional complications love entailed.

Her Christmas wish would never come true.

It was early and the rest of the household still slept when Callum pulled the front door open and stood back for Miranda to pass.

She halted just ahead of him and he heard her gasp as she took in the bright beauty of the morning sunlight on the pristine blanket of fresh-fallen snow.

"This is the gift you said you wanted," he murmured behind her.

"It's so beautiful—so peaceful—it makes my heart hurt." Her voice was husky. "What a perfect start to Christmas Day."

He knew what she meant.

She stepped forward and the sun caught her hair, turning it to gold. Callum followed and her scent stayed with him. Vanilla. And a hint of honey this morning.

"Old Jim will already have put the horses out in the paddock." He led her through the silent, snow-encrusted garden, their Wellingtons crunching on the snow that covered the cobbled pathways.

Mojo and Moxie padded up behind them, looking expectant. Callum eyed the dogs. "You can come but you need to behave. No running off." Opening the gate set in an archway in the stone garden wall, he paused for a moment to let Miranda take in the vista before them.

"Wow." She sounded awed.

"Come on." He snagged her gloved hand in his. "Let me show you."

They entered a lane lined with post-and-rail fencing and leafless trees, their boughs forming ghostly shapes that fragmented the stark landscape.

"It feels like we're the only people in the whole world."

He glanced down at her. "Maybe we are."

With a hint of bravado that had been missing since he'd produced the proof of her father's confession, she said, "You and me? That could be interesting."

"Very," he said drily and watched as color washed her cheeks.

She tried to wiggle her fingers free but he tightened his hold. "There are the horses," he said to distract her.

Followed by the pair of Labradors, they headed for a five-barred gate set in the fence. A rugged-up chestnut came toward them, whickering in greeting, followed by a big bay.

The chestnut nuzzled delicately at Miranda's gloves and she laughed. "This one's gorgeous. What are their names?"

The melancholy that had hung over her yesterday had lifted. Her skin was bright and clear, and a slight flush lay on her cheeks. God, but this woman was gorgeous. His chest squeezed tight.

"The chestnut is Red, the bay Cavalier," he said hastily, before she caught him fawning. "The gray mare at the back is Lady Anne. She's shy. It may take her a while to come forward."

"Oh, I feel so bad—I've got nothing for them."

Callum drew a plastic bag from his coat pocket. "Luckily, I came prepared." He passed her a carrot. Miranda pulled off her glove and tucked it under her other arm. Holding her hand out palm up, she offered the carrot to Red. The chestnut lipped it up.

Cavalier bumped Callum's elbow and he fed the bay a piece, too.

"Here comes Lady Anne," he warned. The gray had edged up on the far side of Miranda.

Miranda stretched her arm out and Lady Anne took the offered morsel. Red's ears went back and the gray mare skittered out of reach with her carrot.

"Not nice, Red," said Miranda reprovingly.

Too soon the carrots were gone.

"I enjoyed that," said Miranda.

Her eyes glowed and Callum's throat grew tight. "At a quieter time, you must come again. We'll go for a ride." The words were out before he could stop them.

She looked as surprised by his impulsive offer as he was.

"That would be nice. Thank you."

She hadn't refused. Callum gave her a broad smile. It gave him a chance to see her again in the New Year, without having to rely on their connection through Adrian. Before she could put her glove back on, Callum snatched her hand. A sizzle of electricity seared him.

"Your fingers are cold."

"Freezing," she said cheerfully.

"I'll warm them." He held her hand between his and gave them a rub, all too conscious of her long fingers dwarfed between his but strong from molding dough. The short, square nails had been painted with clear varnish. Leaning forward, he brushed a kiss over her lips.

They both froze, then broke apart.

Miranda pushed her hair back and Callum stared at her. What was happening? What was her power over him? It was as if he was in the presence of something he'd never felt before—and that he hadn't seen coming.

Ten

The rest of Christmas Day passed in a rush of laughter and joy. Miranda barely had any time alone with Callum, which only reinforced that her decision—not to ruin the day by dwelling on her problems with Flo and Adrian—had been the right one.

After breakfast the family gathered in the living room to open presents beside the Christmas tree. Miranda was astonished to find she was expected to join the family.

Everyone had brought small gifts for each

other. CDs of favorite bands. Books. Aromatherapy lotions. Each carefully chosen. Callum gave her a lacy white apron that made her blush and everyone else giggle, and Miranda was relieved that she'd thought to bring a CD as a gift for him. Thankfully no one had any idea of the significance of his choice.

Her own gift to the family of a selection of small pots of herbs for the kitchen and a huge tin of mouth-watering iced biscuits cut into snowflake shapes was met with cries of delight.

As soon as that was over, Miranda belatedly called Flo and Adrian to wish them a merry Christmas, keeping the conversation deliberately upbeat, then headed for the kitchen. After a hectic, busy morning spent preparing the turkey for the family's Christmas feast that night and the more time-consuming dishes that would be eaten the next day, Miranda whipped up a light lunch of roasted pumpkin soup with pesto and sour cream stirred through, served with freshly baked rolls on the side. It caused oohs of delight. And Miranda flushed with pleasure when Callum's father commented, "You picked a winner, Callum." Her gaze met Callum's then skittered away under the heat and intensity she read there.

Don't make more of it, she warned herself. She was only here because Callum had wanted a date to provide a distraction from Petra's presence tomorrow.

That afternoon she focused on their Christmas dinner, and preparing what could be done in advance for Pauline's party the next day. Although with the help she'd had from Callum's mother as well as Lindsey and Anna, Miranda was starting to feel like a fraud. Even Callum and his brothers wandered in through the course of the afternoon to give a hand, the kitchen ending up full of action and much hilarity. It had been incredibly fun.

The hardest part had been keeping a straight face when Pauline looked around in bewilderment at all the food and demanded, "Who's going to eat all of this? It's far too much."

"Have no fear, Mother," Fraser said. "We're growing men—there won't be a crumb left."

Miranda caught Callum suppressing a grin, and Hunter immediately marched his mother out on the pretext of needing her advice about how to best dry the Italian loafers he'd saturated the previous night.

"You shouldn't have worn them to the carols, Hunter," they heard Pauline say as she followed him out the kitchen, completely diverted.

"You're fortunate to have such a wonderful family," Miranda murmured to Callum.

"I know."

It wasn't only Callum who held Miranda enthralled… she was dangerously close to falling in love with his family.

And that she couldn't afford.

His mother's utter, unfeigned surprise the next day when the first of her birthday guests arrived made the whole loving deception worthwhile, Callum decided as he exchanged looks of satisfaction with his brothers.

"How did I not get the smallest whiff of this?" Pauline asked as cars crowded the forecourt in front of the house.

"It was supposed to be a secret," said Callum.

"Though Dad nearly let the cat out of the bag five minutes after we arrived on Thursday," said Fraser with a mock glare at his father.

"Never could keep a secret, your father." Pauline gave her husband a fond smile, and Callum looked away to give them a private moment.

"I managed to keep it in all of yesterday," said Robin, and everyone laughed.

But when Petra arrived with her father, tension filled the air as Callum stepped closer to Miranda. Petra gave Miranda a quick glance, and aside from the hurt in her eyes, showed little reaction.

But Callum was aware of Miranda shifting away from him, distancing herself. She didn't like the deception he'd asked her to perform, Callum realized.

It grew even more sticky when Callum discovered that Gordon and Petra had been invited to stay with the family for the balance of the weekend and wouldn't be leaving with the other guests.

"Trouble?" Fraser asked a little while later with a meaningful look in Petra's direction.

Callum resisted the urge to snap at his brother. "Nothing I can't handle."

"Good. Because despite the fact that Petra had the sense to dump you, Gordon remains important to our business."

"You invited them to stay?" Callum stared at his brother in disbelief.

"Yes." Fraser narrowed his gaze. "It shouldn't be a problem, should it?"

Callum sincerely hoped it wouldn't become one—but he had already detected Gordon's coolness toward Miranda.

When all the guests had arrived, everyone assembled in the large formal dining for a buffet-style birthday lunch. Callum stopped dead at the sight of Miranda. She'd changed into a red dress that clung softly to her curves. Everything about the dress shrieked *touch me!* He swallowed. How the hell was he supposed to resist such an invitation? In desperation he forced himself to focus on the spread she'd prepared. Miranda

had surpassed herself. An ice sculpture dominated the centre of the table and she'd carried
the winter wonderland theme through in the
snowflake decorations suspended around the
room, with masses of tall, white tapered candles
lit to give an impression of glittering Christmas
tree lights.

After lunch Pauline opened her gifts, and with
every card she read out, her eyes grew increasingly dewy. Callum was surprised to see
Miranda hand his mother a box lightly wrapped
in tissue paper.

"Happy birthday," Miranda said.

His mother pulled off the wrapping to reveal
a half dozen brandy snaps filled with cream, and
a finger lick at the end of one had her whimper-
ing with delight.

It stunned Callum that Miranda had taken the
care to make the sweet he'd told her his mother
loved. But her consideration warmed his heart.
For an instant he was guiltily conscious of the
fact that she should be spending Christmas with
her own mother and brother—not his.

* * *

As the afternoon passed, Miranda was supremely aware of Callum's every move whenever they were together, and she grew increasingly uncomfortable with the number of times his fingers would brush hers, or his hand would settle on her waist, the fine, soft jersey fabric of her dress failing to present any substantial barrier to the warmth of his touch. She knew he was making certain that Gordon harbored no hopes of a reconciliation between his daughter and Callum. But she disliked the deceit and the flare of pain in Petra's eyes. And on top of that, it troubled her deeply that she was deceiving Callum. He still had no idea of the damage Adrian had done to an Ironstone car…and more significantly that she hadn't disclosed it to him.

Yet how could she? She couldn't have gone against Adrian's wishes. And ultimately it was Adrian's problem. How would he ever learn to take responsibility for his life if she fixed all his problems for him? Look what a mess Flo made simply because she expected everyone to leap around and fix things for her. Her father treating Flo as a china doll had only worsened the problem.

But now Christmas was over. Adrian's worry about being locked up over the holiday with little chance of bail was no longer valid. And every time her gaze connected with Callum's, Miranda wished she hadn't agreed to keep quiet until she returned to London. As much as she hadn't wanted to raise something controversial on Christmas Day or his mother's birthday, she now needed Callum to be in the picture.

Then maybe they could finally advance their strained relationship. But would he still even want to be friends when he found out she'd deceived him?

Tea had been served in delicate china cups. Miranda sneaked out to take a five-minute break in the downstairs study and decided she would call Adrian. Maybe he would agree to let her tell Callum the truth—presuming she got the opportunity.

Adrian answered his mobile on first ring. "What's up, sis?"

She told him, and when he spoke again the breezy note had vanished. "No," he said adamantly. "I'll tell him when I'm ready."

"On Monday when I get back, you said," she reminded him.

"Maybe."

He was trying to wriggle off the hook. Her brother must be truly scared of the consequences.

"It's not going to get easier—and if you leave it too long, I'll tell him myself."

"I know that." Adrian sounded so despondent she felt like an absolute witch. Then he said, "I've been getting threatening calls. I've managed to put them off because I told them you were away."

"It doesn't make any difference whether I'm there or not. I've told you—they're not getting my money. Absolutely not." She breathed deeply. "Look, Callum will give you a break."

Adrian's sin wasn't anything like what their

father had done. They couldn't use that as a yardstick for judging Callum's likely reaction. "I'm sure Callum will understand." Miranda hoped that he would live up to her brave claim.

Adrian muttered something she was grateful she couldn't make out, and then hung up.

Well, she'd handled that just beautifully!

"Why the frown?"

She started at the sound of Callum's voice and discovered he was standing in front of her. Had he overheard her conversation? She hoped not.

She forced a smile. "Nothing much."

"You were on the phone. Trouble? Is it your mother again?"

At least Callum hadn't homed in on Adrian. "A little."

"She takes advantage of you." Callum held her gaze.

"And you," she said.

"And me," he conceded. "We're not doing her any favors. By always fixing her problems, we've allowed her to become totally irresponsible."

Miranda had reached that conclusion herself, but it still stung to hear it from Callum. It took sheer willpower to stop herself from defending Flo.

"I suppose I should butt out," he said when she didn't answer.

"No, you're quite right. I need to stand up to her."

There was sympathy in his eyes. "It won't be easy."

That was an understatement. Flo was going to rail against it, Miranda suspected. "No, it won't be easy. And I don't want to hurt her feelings."

"Sometimes one has to be cruel to be kind," said Callum.

And Miranda suspected he was thinking not of Flo—but Petra.

After seeing the last of the guests off, Callum and his brothers trooped back into the house with his parents. Gordon had gone up to his room already.

His mother had been thrilled by the unexpected party and was still looking over-whelmed. "I should check on—"

"The kitchen is fine," his father said firmly. "There are four women taking care of it, and one is a trained chef."

"Then I suppose we can go to bed, then."

Callum pecked his mother good-night on the cheek, and wasn't surprised when his father quickly followed her up the stairs. He had a feeling his father was going to reap the benefits of the celebration.

A lull fell over the big house. Anna, Petra and Lindsey were helping Miranda tidy up, and his brothers had gone out to the stables to feed and rug up the horses, because Old Jim had gone home to spend the day with his even more elderly mother.

So Callum made his way to the kitchen to find Miranda. There had been worry in her eyes earlier—he wanted to check that she was okay. And he wanted to make sure that putting her into close proximity with Petra hadn't made her too uncomfortable. She clearly didn't like the deceit—despite his explanation that by his dating another woman, Gordon would forget all thoughts of a match between him and Petra.

Or at least that's what he told himself right up until the moment he reached the kitchen and halted in the doorway.

She'd pulled a long double-breasted white chef's jacket on over the red touch-me dress. He supposed he should be grateful that she wasn't wearing the sexy apron he'd given her…

Seeing her rubbing down the black granite bench tops and steel-fronted appliances reminded him of the night in his town house and involuntarily his body hardened.

Even wearing that jacket, she was the sexiest woman he'd ever known.

He stuck his hands in his trouser pockets and glanced around. There was no sign of Petra— or his brothers' girlfriends—so he sauntered forward. "Hey, Cinderella, looks like the elves have been busy."

"You're mixing Christmas with fairy tales."

"What's wrong with that?"

She thought for a moment. "Nothing."

"Where are Petra, Lindsey and Anna?" he asked.

"Probably in the bath by now—where all good princesses should be." She smiled at him—and a blast of heat spread through him to settle low in his belly, building mercilessly on the arousal he already felt. "I think they're both a bit shell-shocked by how tired you can get just from standing on your feet all day. I'm used to it," she added quickly.

"Come and sit with me—I might even rub your poor abused feet." He shot her a smoldering look from under heavy eyelids and watched with satisfaction as she colored.

Freeing his hands from his pockets, Callum led an unusually pliant Miranda into the sitting room, where flames licked at the logs in the grate and the lights of the Christmas tree twinkled.

He paused to fill up two glasses with tawny port and crossed to where she'd sunk down on the squashy couch with her feet tucked under her, the folds of the dress draped around her.

She looked so right here in his family home. His family liked her, he could tell. By the way Fraser teased her. By the way his mother had almost burst into tears when Miranda had given her the brandy snaps.

She fitted in.

He'd almost forgotten the deception of her accompanying him as a "fake" date. It felt so real.

When he'd decided weeks ago to help her attain her dream—and more financial independence—it had been so he could salve his conscience. He hadn't expected the hunger that ate him every time he looked at her. He hadn't expected to like her. And he certainly hadn't expected his family to be so charmed by her.

When had his connection to her started to become so…emotional?

"What is it?" Miranda had taken a sip of the sweet port, but now she examined him standing in front of her, his legs apart, and male enough to make her forget all about the rich, nutty flavor of the liqueur that had delighted her only seconds earlier.

Callum wore a strange, bemused expression. The intensity in his eyes unfurled a restlessness deep within her.

He shook his head and laughed. "I think I'm going crazy."

"You? Crazy?" She raised an eyebrow. "Never."

But he didn't laugh as she'd intended. Instead he stared at her until she shifted under that intimidating gaze.

"What is it that makes me forget about everything else when you're around?"

"Now it's *my* fault you're going crazy?" She tried to laugh again, but found that her voice had dried up. His admission made her toes curl.

"Maybe not." He crossed to a wall unit, where he pulled a drawer open and extracted a box. "You said once that your only weakness is dark chocolate."

Her gaze lingered on Callum's broad shoulders and trailed down to the long legs clad in dark trousers. Chocolate was no longer her only weakness....

"I couldn't eat another thing," she protested as he came toward her brandishing a bar of Lindt.

"Indulge me." He tore the wrapper off. "Have you ever tasted dark chocolate and port together?"

Wordlessly, she shook her head.

"Then you haven't lived."

His voice was deep and throaty, and Miranda's pulse went through the roof.

"Open your mouth."

She never considered not obeying. Her lips parted. He placed a morsel on her tongue and the chocolate melted in her mouth. It tasted sublime.

"Now the port."

He held the glass for her, and Miranda set her lips to the rim. Their eyes locked. He tipped the glass ever so slightly. The liquid mingled in her mouth with the rich sweet and flavor exploded on her tongue.

Callum set the glass down, and when he

leaned forward to stroke her hair back from her face with gentle hands, her heart dropped.

"It's been way too long since I've kissed you, Miranda."

The moment had finally arrived. He'd brushed her lips too briefly yesterday morning during their walk, leaving her hungering for more. All day yesterday and today she'd waited, tension winding up within her.

Which made her feel even worse about not telling him about Adrian. He'd done so much to help her family, and all they'd been was Trouble with a capital *T*.

"You're not going to stop me this time, are you?"

Was she so obvious? Tongue-tied, she shook her head.

"Good," he purred.

His lips were firm on hers. He pulled her up against him and she became aware of the power of his body under the cotton shirt. His arms were strong around her.

He was all man.

She parted her lips and he devoured her. All *hungry* male. He gave a groan that turned her weak. She wanted him.

"That's how to taste dark chocolate." He brushed a kiss over her lips. "But if we continue this, someone might walk in on us." His laugh was breathless. "My brothers only went to feed the horses. One of them could return any second."

She ran her fingertips over his jaw, pausing to rest them against the soft pad of his lower lip. His eyes ignited with passion and he sucked a finger into his mouth, his tongue swirling around it.

Her breathing quickened.

Removing her hand, he took her mouth, plundering it, filling every crevice with his tongue. He tasted of port, chocolate and aroused male, and when he'd finished, he lifted his head and she gazed into eyes heavy with desire.

"I don't want to wait anymore." His voice was hoarse. "Come up to my room with me."

Unable to speak, she nodded.

* * *

Callum shoved his bedroom door shut with his foot, and—holding Miranda's gaze—locked the door.

Her pupils darkened, consuming the caramel gold of her irises, and causing his body to shudder and harden in anticipation.

He shrugged his tie off, crossed the room, and dropped the tie across the railing of his huge four-poster bed.

Miranda followed more slowly.

He waited for her, unbuttoning his shirt. She stopped at the bottom of the bed, her eyes huge.

The edges of his shirt fell open. He reached for her and brought her close. Letting his fingers caress her nape, he speared them into the silken mass of hair and tilted her head back. Scanning her features, he saw no sign of resistance.

He had her. Alone. At last.

With a sigh of relief he unbuttoned the double row of buttons and pushed the chef's jacket from her shoulders. His shirt, trousers, underpants and her sinful dress all followed, then he tumbled back onto the bed, taking her with him. She landed sprawled, all soft skin and tousled curls against his nakedness.

A moan of satisfaction shook him. "Kiss me, Miranda."

She obliged, and her hair caressed him, tresses scented with the vanilla that teased his dreams. He played his hands over her shoulders, along her back, and his fingers encountered her bra strap. He undid the clasp. She lifted her torso, and as the halter-neck bra fell away she wriggled free.

Callum gasped.

Her breasts hung above him. Full, ripe curves that tempted him to touch…to taste.

He reached out reverently and caressed the berry nubs with gentle fingers. She arched sharply, and a keening sound broke from her throat. Seeking to taste her, he closed his mouth around the dark tip and sucked it. It hardened further, and he knew she was as desperate for him as he for her.

Keeping his mouth on her breast, he slid a hand

down over the swell of her stomach and dipped between her legs—and found her moist and ready.

Before he could take the next step, her legs wrapped around his hips and she pushed herself upright, breaking the contact of his mouth on her.

Miranda rubbed herself along the rigid length of his erection. Callum nearly came apart. Only a brief bit of satin separated them from the final sweet connection they both sought. Impatiently he pushed the thin thong of her panties aside and, the delicate barrier gone, she sank down on him.

Pure ecstasy.

He growled in delight. Miranda moved above him and heat consumed him in a bright white flash. Clasping his hands over her hips, he fought to control the pace. But when she bent forward and outlined his mouth with her tongue, laving his lips, Callum moaned, his resolve crumbling. Then she sealed the caress with a kiss. And all the while he drove fiercely, desperately upward into her.

Callum shuddered, his body full of tension. She fell forward, boneless, breathless, on top of his chest, her hair silky against his cheeks, her fragrance embracing him.

And the heat exploded around them, tumbling them into the hot vortex of desire.

Eleven

Callum woke to a sense of supreme satisfaction.

Miranda lay curled up beside him under the covers, one hand resting on his bare chest, spreading warmth through him. It felt so right. Her hand belonged there, against his skin. Over his heart. He wanted to wake every morning to her touch, to the softness of her body tucked against his, her golden hair tousled around her face.

She was his.

The strength of emotion that surged through

him awed him. Reaching out, he brushed a silky curl away from her cheek. She stirred.

Her eyes opened, and in the pale morning light that spilled through his bedroom window Callum saw something warm and wonderful in their golden-brown depths. Then alarm took over, chasing the glow out and filling her eyes with shadows.

She was about to withdraw from him. He couldn't—wouldn't—allow that to happen. Not after last night.

"Don't move," he demanded.

She blinked up at him. "Why?"

"Because I want to look at you."

Miranda gave a breathy laugh and shifted away, leaving a cold space in the bed beside him.

"You're making me feel uncomfortable."

"Don't feel uncomfortable." He rolled closer and cupped his hand under her chin, forcing her to meet his gaze. "You better get used to it. I'll never tire of looking at you."

Something flickered in the caramel eyes that melted his heart. "Oh, yes, you will."

He shook his head. "No, I won't." *Not ever.* But he wasn't ready to confess that yet. Instead he let his fingertips caress the soft skin of her cheek. "What we had last night…I want more."

Yet he couldn't put the unfamiliar emotions and desires that churned inside him into words. All he knew was that he wanted to savor this…thing…that bound them together. Driven by an impulse, he leaned forward and pressed his lips fiercely against hers, determined to make her acknowledge the power of his need.

Last night's wild heat returned in a rush. Swirling through him, racing through his bloodstream, quickening the passion that had ignited at the first touch of his lips to hers. Her lips parted, his tongue plundered the warm depths of her mouth.

And words became unnecessary.

It was the sound of the dogs barking, a shout from Hunter and the lilt of feminine laughter outside that brought Callum abruptly back to his senses. He stared down at the woman who had made him forget everything. His family. His work. He caught sight of the clock on the bed stand. Even the time.

He gave a husky laugh. "My God, I was ready to take you again."

She was breathing quickly, and her eyes had gone dark with desire. The covers had shifted, revealing a pale, creamy shoulder and the slope of one breast. Want surged through him, and he hauled in a ragged breath.

"We better get up." With heavy reluctance he sat up and shrugged the bedclothes off. "Breakfast will be ready—and I don't want anyone coming searching for us." He wanted to keep the intimate joy he'd found with Miranda a secret from the world.

"No, we don't want that."

Miranda moved away, and this time he let her. Her cheeks were stained a rosy pink from the kiss they'd shared, and she took care to keep her nakedness covered. "Your mother told me she was old-fashioned, and didn't approve of us sharing rooms. I feel like I've abused her trust."

There was a strange expression in her eyes.

Callum resisted the impulse to pull her back into his arms, tumble her against the rumpled sheets and possess her with the desire that burned so hotly within him. Instead he said, "I wouldn't worry too much about that. My mother will be only too pleased that I've found someone."

Uncertainty glimmered in her eyes. "I don't want to deceive your mother—your family—any further."

"I wouldn't ask that of you."

Her shoulders stiffened, and her eyes grew wary. "So what are you asking?"

Callum hesitated. Hell, what was he asking? For a moment fear closed around him. He shook it away. This was no time to get cold feet. But he tempered what he meant to say. "I want to make this fake relationship real."

He thought he glimpsed joy in the gold-brown eyes. Too quickly it was gone. For a moment he thought she was going to object. Then she smiled. "I'd like that, too."

An overwhelming relief settled over him. Miranda hadn't refused outright as he'd half expected. She had said yes.

And he had no intention of letting her escape.

Miranda floated downstairs after a quick stop at her room to pull on something more suitable than the red halter-neck dress she'd been wearing last night. She was unable to suppress the silly smile that curved her lips, all too conscious of the man padding down the stairs beside her, his fingers loosely linked with hers.

No doubt she was heading for heartbreak, falling for Callum. It was stupid. Totally insane. Yet she couldn't help herself.

And she would allow herself no regrets.

This was her last chance to seize a slice of happiness for herself. It wouldn't last. But she would enjoy it while it did. Because it would be over too soon—she knew that. As surely as she knew that Callum Ironstone would not fall in love with someone like her. He would find someone with the class and the social connections he needed. Not an embezzler's daughter living under the fog of her father's notoriety.

They entered the dining room, and her gaze settled on Petra. Someone like Petra Harris.

The blonde glanced across at them.

Miranda read the bruised hurt in Petra's pale eyes as she took in their interlinked fingers. For Petra it had never been about business interests. The woman really had loved Callum, she realized. Then her gaze shifted to the man seated beside Petra at the breakfast table. She took in Gordon Harris's tight lips. For Petra's father it had been about business. And he looked none too pleased.

Hunter greeted them first. "We started without you. Mother decided you two must've gone for a walk again and lost track of time."

Miranda felt herself grow red. Thankfully Pauline wasn't in the dining room, and she didn't have to answer any polite questions about how their walk had gone. She didn't dare look at Callum as he held a chair out for her before sliding into the empty seat at her side.

"I promised to take Lindsey down to the craft fair in the village." Jack rose to his feet.

"Can we go, too?" Anna turned to Hunter. "Please?"

Hunter rolled his eyes. "What have you got me into?" he demanded of his brother as he pushed his chair back.

Within minutes the dining room had emptied. Only the Harrises—and Fraser—remained.

"Gordon wants to schedule some time with you this morning, Callum," Fraser told his brother as he, too, got to his feet.

"We can talk after breakfast," replied Callum, lifting a pot of aromatic coffee. After Petra had refused the offer of a cup, he said, "Coffee, Miranda? Or would you prefer tea?"

Or me?

Miranda could've sworn the invitation was in his wickedly glinting eyes. "Coffee," she said huskily, all too conscious of the effect he had on her as he filled first her cup then his.

Gordon's mouth was suddenly grim. "After breakfast will do. I was starting to think you might be otherwise occupied." He glanced meaningfully at Miranda.

Callum stilled, then carefully set the coffee-pot down.

Petra put a hand on her father's arm. "Daddy—"

"No, Petra." Gordon shook his daughter's hand off. He turned in his seat. "Callum, I had hoped the relationship between our families would be more than business. I had hoped…" He paused.

"Daddy, *please.*"

Petra looked mortified. A shaft of pity for the other woman pierced Miranda. Wasn't it enough that she was hurting already? Did her father have to humiliate her, too?

She shot Callum a pleading look. Couldn't he do anything to stop this? His arm came across the back of her chair, and his hand rested possessively on her shoulders. "Gordon, I think—"

"Petra would make you a very suitable wife. Much better than *she* ever would."

The anger in his gaze stupefied Miranda.

"I can't believe that you broke it off with Petra for *her.* Think whose daughter she is. The fruit doesn't fall far from the vine. Will you ever be able to trust her?"

"Daddy!"

Callum's body had coiled tight, and Miranda could feel the tension radiating from him. Suddenly she felt decidedly ill.

"Yes, I can trust her," Callum bit out.

Oh, heavens. Miranda grew cold. *Trust her?*

Callum's free fist hit the edge of the table with a loud bang. Both Miranda and Petra jumped. Callum glared at Gordon. "Frankly, I wasn't intending to spend the morning closeted in meetings. And, yes, I had intended to spend the day with Miranda, who is one of the nicest women I've ever had the fortune of dating."

Miranda sighed. Poor Petra.

"So you can be the first to congratulate us, Gordon."

"First to congratulate you?"

Gordon's shocked expression echoed Miranda's own shock.

Callum's hand tightened on her shoulder. "We're getting married."

"Married?" A gasp of delight came from the door.

Miranda closed her eyes as Pauline hurled herself across the room.

"Oh, Callum, I heard a thump and thought something must have broken. But this is wonderful. Just wait until I tell your father."

Oh, help. What in heaven's name had Callum done?

As Callum closed the door of the study behind them ten minutes later, Miranda wrenched herself out of his hold. "What possessed you to say such a dumb thing to Gordon in there? I feel like such a fool."

"Hey, it's not that bad," he said, the protective streak that he hadn't known existed still strong as he crossed the room to stand beside her. "I—"

"I told you that I didn't want to lie any further to your family." She covered her face with her hands and her curls bobbed. "Now your parents think we're getting married. At least your brothers haven't heard. You can tell *them* it's a stupid misunderstanding."

"Why?" Callum could see his bald question had thrown her.

She dropped her hands and stared at him. "Your parents like me. Once they hear that you only said it to protect me from Gordon's nastiness, they'll understand." Then her mouth formed an *O*. "Of course, you can't do that, can you? Gordon is an important shareholder. That's the whole reason your brought me along this weekend—to stop exactly the kind of scenario that just occurred in the dining room from taking place."

Callum crossed the distance between them in two long strides. Catching her by her shoulders, he growled down at her. "Listen to me. I wouldn't allow anyone to talk to you like that—and I don't care that he's a shareholder."

She tipped her head back. "That's very noble, but—"

"It's not noble. I—"

He stilled. He'd almost said, *I want to marry you.*

Callum froze. He couldn't propose marriage just to stop Miranda feeling humiliated by Gordon's attack—even though he'd been tempted to punch the man in the jaw instead of banging the table.

Yet in the past he'd asked her to marry him to be his hostess....

That reason was no better. Damn it, he wanted her to marry him for himself.

The bombshell thought shocked him rigid.

Why?

Because she was special. Like no other woman he'd ever met.

"Of course it was noble." She was looking at him like he'd done something heroic.

He shook his head to clear it. "I was angry. He was insulting you."

"No one has ever defended me like that before."

He didn't suppose they had. Miranda had always protected her mother and brother. There'd been no one to protect her. His chest expanded with emotion. "That's about to change."

She laughed, and the bittersweet sound caught at his gut.

"Callum, he didn't say anything that both you and I know isn't true. Petra would make you a fabulous wife. And given the fact that my father stole from you, then committed suicide, it's true that will make me a scandalous girlfriend."

"That doesn't matter."

"It does matter." Her eyes had gone dark. "And how can you trust me?"

"Miranda—"

A knock sounded on the door.

Callum marched over and yanked it open. "What?" he demanded of Fraser.

"Have you seen Petra?"

"No," he snapped, and started to close the door in Fraser's face.

His brother stuck a foot in the crack. "You let me believe she broke it off with you."

"Not now." He glared at this brother. "Leave us in peace."

Fraser removed his foot, and this time Callum closed the door with a determined thud.

Miranda had moved to the window. She stood looking at the view over Lake Windermere down at the bottom of the property, the sag of her shoulders revealing how troubled she was.

Tenderness filled him. "Stop fretting."

She turned to meet his gaze over her shoulder. "Trust me, I have reason to fret. Every single thing that Gordon said was true." She shook her head as she started to object. "I like your parents so much. I was looking forward to coming back with you, riding the horses." She gestured at the paddocks visible to one side of the house.

At the yearning in her voice, cold fingers of dread danced over his skin.

Did he want this? A woman who loved his horses, his home, his family…but not him? Out in the corner of the paddock he could see Red pawing through the snow. In a flash of insight he saw what marrying him would mean—it would give Miranda back everything she'd lost and finally assuage his guilt.

And he'd get the woman he wanted more than he'd ever wanted anything in his life.

Callum sucked in a breath. He crossed the room, and slid his arms around her shoulders from behind and drew her to his chest.

Beneath his palms the woolen cardigan she wore was soft, and he could feel the rise and fall of her rib cage as she breathed. His fingers crept forward. Below the cardigan, the edge of her wraparound dress had parted and his fingertips brushed her bare skin. Need swamped him. *God.* Just by breathing she made him desire her. He resisted the fierce urge to yank her up against his hardening body. Now was not the time.

The thought he'd had when he'd woken with her in his arms this morning returned.

This woman belonged with him.

He stared blindly over her shoulder at a red-breasted robin chirping in the undergrowth beneath the window.

If she married him, he would have her in his bed each night instead of seeing her only through functions she catered for him—or through communications about her brother. Surely this was a win-win situation?

So why wasn't he asking, begging, her to marry him?

Because this wasn't what he wanted.

He wanted Miranda to love him.

And there was no chance of that ever happening.

With a hop, the robin he'd been staring at vanished into the undergrowth, bringing Callum back to life. His hands dropped from her shoulders. He felt the loss of the softness of her skin acutely.

He loved her.

God.

Despite the success of his parents' marriage he'd always known that love wasn't easy or straightforward, and that it would make an emotional mess of him—and he'd been right. Good thing she didn't know how he felt.

But he had to ask again. Give her the opportunity to accept what he could give her. Because then he'd get what he wanted more than life. Her.

Callum drew a shuddering breath. "Miranda, you really could marry me—and make my dumb suggestion a reality." He directed the words at golden curls that cascaded down the back of her head, relieved he didn't have to meet her eyes. This way she would never know how desperately he craved to hear her say yes. "We would go downstairs and celebrate our engagement. What do you say?"

Miranda spun around.

Callum was asking her to marry him? There was an expression in his eyes that caused her heart to ache.

A flutter of hope made her stretch out her hand to touch his chest—to check he was real, that this wasn't a dream.

The tension of the moment was shattered by the jazzy "Jingle Bells" ringtone of her phone in her cardigan pocket. Definitely no dream. Life had intruded.

Miranda hesitated. It might be Adrian, calling her back after terminating their call yesterday, but she didn't want to speak to him. Not now, not while Callum was asking her to marry him. Not when she knew Gordon was right. She had been less than trustworthy. Her stomach clenched.

"Answer it."

Reluctantly she hauled it out of her pocket, but by that time the ringing had stopped. She stared at the screen and her heart sank. "It was Adrian."

"Do you want to call him back?"

She shook her head. "I called him yesterday—he's probably just returning my call." No point telling Callum her brother had hung up on her because she'd wanted permission to tell Callum the truth.

As she was about to pocket the phone, it started to ring again, loud and intrusive. Faced with no choice under Callum's expectant gaze, she answered it.

Impatient now, Callum thrust his hands into the pockets of his trousers and turned away to stare back out the window, trying not to listen to Miranda's conversation with her brother. He searched for the robin but couldn't find it.

Miranda was going to accept his proposal. He'd seen it in her eyes.

The corners of his mouth turned up as he anticipated Fraser's surprise. Callum would be the first of the Ironstones to marry. For once he would've beaten his brothers at something life-changing. There was some small masculine satisfaction in that.

Behind him Miranda's voice lowered, catching his attention.

"I can't talk about that, Adrian. Not now."

What was going on? What did she need to speak to her brother about that she couldn't say in front of him?

Frowning slightly, he swiveled to face her.

She gave him a fleeting, sideways glance from beneath those long, dark lashes and turned away. "Thank you for that. I appreciate it more than I can tell you." A silence. Then, "Yes, I know it's hard for you, but it has to be done. I must go. I'll call you later."

Was Adrian in some kind of trouble? Callum told himself the suspicion was unfounded.

Except…there was that air of discomfort.

When she clicked the phone shut he asked, driven by a compulsion he couldn't name, "What's wrong?"

Her lashes fluttered down. She drew a deep breath, looked up and said in a rush, "Adrian's being blackmailed."

Twelve

"**W**hat?" Callum's eyebrows jerked together into a ferocious frown. "What do you mean Adrian's being blackmailed?"

Miranda forced herself to hold his gaze. Inside she was trembling. *I can trust her.* Callum's words rang in her ears. He wouldn't want anything to do with her after this. She wouldn't blame him for reneging on his proposal.

"The day you called me to see you, I found out after our meeting that Adrian had crashed—" she hesitated "—a car."

"Yes?"

"I didn't want to tell you because you'd said you were pleased with him." Miranda spread her hands in a gesture of helplessness. "I was afraid it would jeopardize his chances of getting a great reference from a vacation job."

"But what does that have to do his job? Or being blackmailed? Was someone killed? Did he fail to report it?" Callum looked bewildered.

"No, no one died." Thank heavens! "But he'd borrowed the car without permission." She bit her lip. "It was one of your company's cars."

Callum's eyes turned to slits. "Why didn't he tell me?"

"He was scared you would fire him…and have him arrested and charged with theft."

He didn't blink.

Unnerved by the relentless stare, she blurted out, "So he found a panel beater who could fix the car in a hurry and managed to get it back into the car yard before anyone noticed."

Still Callum said nothing.

Miranda started to tremble. "And now the

panel beater says if Adrian doesn't pay him more, the man is going to blow the whistle on Adrian and tell his supervisor."

"And you've known about this all the time?"

The lethally soft tone caused Miranda's throat to close. She nodded, unable to speak.

His relentless blue eyes bored into hers. "You believed I would have had him arrested?"

She thought about that. Did she really believe he would have Adrian arrested?

"You've done it before," she pointed out in her own defense. But her father's crime had been so much worse. "And you must remember I believed that you'd had no reason back then. And this time I knew Adrian had actually taken—" she couldn't bring herself to say *stolen* "—your car. At the start I didn't think you'd have any compassion for him."

Callum turned away. "Thanks for the vote of confidence."

Had that been pain she'd glimpsed in his eyes?

But that would have to mean that she was capable of hurting him and she knew she wasn't.

He saw her merely as someone who would make his business life easier—a memory from the night before came to her—and someone he desired.

She blinked back the tears that threatened. This wasn't going to work out. Ever. Better she cut her losses and leave.

"So I suppose that means you aren't going to marry me after all." His mouth was compressed.

"I don't think it would ever work," she said, and the ache of loss spread through her, drowning her in sadness.

The drive back to London took forever.

Miranda was conscious of Callum's hands gripping the steering wheel. They'd stopped twice—briefly—but neither lingered; both of them were eager to get back to London.

There was a constant ache below Miranda's heart. Christmas was over. And so was any brief accord she and Callum had shared. Heaven help her, she'd enjoyed playing Callum's girlfriend. She had come so close to a chance to make it real. And she suspected the ache eventuated from her knowledge that it could never be real. Any relationship between her and Callum had been doomed before it could get started.

Finally the car turned into the narrow street where she lived. As soon as it drew to a halt, Miranda leaped out. "Thanks—"

But Callum was already at the trunk, taking out her overnight bag and the baskets, now filled with a collection of empty containers and kitchen-ware.

"Let me take that." He relieved her of the handle of her overnight bag. At the top of the steps, he paused. "Miranda—"

The door swung open and Flo fell out, her eyes wild. "Oh, darling, I'm so glad you're here. Adrian is in such trouble. He's taken my car to sell it because he needs to get his hands on some cash."

Nosing his car into one of London's seedier suburbs the morning of Boxing Day, Callum was grateful for being given the opportunity to talk some sense into young Adrian's head— when they finally found him. They'd driven around London most of last night and been unable to locate Flo's car, either with or without Adrian in it.

Miranda was beside herself. "What if he's hurt?" She unfolded arms that she'd folded less than a minute ago. "This man's a criminal. He might kill Adrian. Though I might just kill him myself," she said darkly. "What is he thinking?"

He glanced at her. "We'll find Adrian. There are only so many places that'll be open today where he could sell the car. But surely Adrian doesn't think that'll make this blackmail problem go away? He'll have to keep paying this crook money forever."

"That's what I told him." She looked utterly miserable, curled up in the passenger seat. "But he still didn't want me to tell you. He hero-worships you, you know. I should have taken matters out of his hands and told you earlier— but I didn't want him to end up like Mum, evading responsibility for his actions, getting someone else to do the dirty work. I'd already had to find the money for the panel beater the first time. So I told him I wouldn't give him any more money, thinking that would mean he'd have to tell you. But all he did was keep putting it off—and beg me not to tell you. I never thought of him trying to sell Mum's car."

If he could get his hands on her brother right now all hero worship would end. Didn't Adrian realize what he was doing to his sister?

He could understand why she hadn't dobbed Adrian in—she had a fierce loyalty to her family and she was right about it being Adrian's job to 'fess up. None of this could have been easy on her. He said, "We'll find him. He'll be okay."

Whether Adrian would still be fine after Callum had gotten through tearing a strip off his hide was quite another matter.

"You must be regretting giving Adrian that job." It was four hours later and Miranda knew Callum must be gnashing his teeth, but he showed no sign of it as they pulled up at their third car fair, facing the now-familiar sight of hundreds of cars being examined by backpackers and students all looking for a bargain. And the equally familiar trawl up and down the lines in the slanting drizzle, searching for Flo's Kia.

Except this time they found it in the second row.

When Adrian saw them approaching, his shoulders sagged. "I suppose I've wrecked my chances of ever landing that scholarship now?" he said to Callum as the three of them huddled under the shade cloth.

"You should have come and told me—young men often do silly things."

Adrian flushed under the older man's scrutiny.

"Do you realize how much worry you've caused your sister?" Callum put his hands on his hips and stared Adrian down. "She's got enough on her plate without having to run after you all the time."

Her brother looked sheepish. "I didn't think."

"No, I don't suppose you did. Nor did you think when you rushed off with your mother's car. You're going to be going off to university or to work and you're going to leave your mother—and sister—without a car?"

Adrian lowered his gaze and stared at the floor, thoroughly chastened.

After a pause he looked up and met Miranda's sympathetic eyes. "I'm sorry, sis. I shouldn't have done it." Turning to Callum, he asked, "What will you do about—"

"About the reparation for the car you crashed?"

Adrian swallowed, and his eyes flickered nervously from side to side. "Uh, yes."

Callum inspected Adrian, then said, "I have a social welfare project I'm putting together—I'd like you to be involved."

Adrian looked astonished. "Me?"

"Yes." Callum started to smile. "I rather suspect that you're going to have a busy year. I know that the scholarships committee is going to want to meet you. You're going to have to work hard to impress them. I can't get you in on my recommendation alone."

Adrian appeared about to fall down with relief. "Oh, no, I understand that. I'll do my best."

"Good."

That one word told Miranda of the high expectations Callum had of her brother. Her
brother would be in good hands—the best.

Flo nearly wept when Callum, Miranda and
Adrian returned to the little terrace house with
her car. But it became clear that Callum had
plans for her, too.

"Miranda is going to be very busy with her
new business." He gave Flo a meaningful stare.
"She's going to need help."

"I can help."

Miranda started to object. What could Flo
do—aside from spend money like water? But
Callum held up a hand, halting what she'd been
about to say.

"I could help her with baking—as I did last
week."

That was true, her mother had been a great
help in the time leading up to Pauline's birthday.

"You could also probably take charge of
hiring the crockery, cutlery and glasses that
Miranda needs."

"Yes, yes." Flo looked animated. "I know a

couple of places that would give me very good deals."

Callum was brilliant.

Miranda could see what he was doing: giving her mother's life meaning. And giving her responsibility. If it worked, it would be fantastic.

Callum had insisted on taking Miranda out for dinner. She needed a break from the mayhem that her family had caused. And afterward he took her to his town house for coffee.

The lights were blinking on the Christmas tree in the drawing room, giving his home a welcoming ambience after the cold and drizzle of the day. As they sat in two comfortable armchairs in front of a roaring fire, their cups of coffee untouched, Miranda said apologetically for the umpteenth time, "I'm terribly sorry for all the inconvenience my family has caused you."

He waved a dismissive hand, not wanting her to take responsibility for her mother and brother. "Don't worry about it. Everything is sorted out."

She gave him a hesitant smile. "Not quite everything."

"What have I overlooked?"

"I never answered your question."

"Which one?"

But he knew.

Miranda looked suddenly anxious, and tension filled him.

"You mean my will-you-marry-me question?" he asked, on the remote chance he'd gotten it wrong.

For a second he thought she was going to turn and run. But she stayed. Her chin went up. "Is it still open for consideration?"

"I thought you said it would never work."

She lifted her chin. "It will work. We'll make it work. I want to marry you."

"You want to marry me? Why?"

"Why do you think?"

Callum started to enjoy himself. "Because I have a family you like?"

Her teeth snapped shut. "No."

"Because I have a country house you like… which even has horses?"

He knew the moment she sensed that he was teasing. The caramel-colored eyes he loved so much began to sparkle. "No—but I definitely want to visit again."

"It must be because I lust after your body?"

She swallowed. "We-ll, that might be part of it."

"Or because I love you?"

"What?" Her eyes went wide.

"I love you." He started to laugh. "Don't you know that by now?"

"I hoped but…I wasn't sure."

"Of course I love you—I think the whole world knows it."

"How long…?"

"Well, it certainly wasn't the first time I met you."

"Nor the time I responded to your summons," she said firmly.

"I just wanted to get that girl who'd called me a murderer off my conscience. But I hadn't anticipated the effect a grown-up Miranda would have on my libido." He rose to his feet and pulled her out of the armchair into his arms.

Miranda's eyebrows lowered as she peered up at him. "You nearly married another woman."

"Almost," he said, grinning unrepentantly down at the woman he held in his arms, "but I didn't. Actually, that was when I fell in love with you, though I didn't realize it at the time. I just knew there was no way I could marry Petra—anyone—when all I could think about was you. It was only later that I realized it was love."

"Look." Miranda pointed. "Is that what I think it is?"

Callum peered up. "It's mistletoe."

"I thought so," she said with supreme satisfaction.

His arms came around her. "You don't need an excuse to kiss me. Just do it anytime you want."

She linked her arms around his neck and drew his head down.

"I fully intend to kiss you plenty. Because I love you, too," she whispered against his mouth, thankful that all her Christmas wishes had been fulfilled.

Callum Ironstone would forever be her Christmas love.

* * * * *